CW00916901

# The Price
## of
## Poppies

by

Susan M Cowley

# THE PRICE OF POPPIES

# Acknowledgments

My inspiration to write this book came when I discovered my great great Uncle, Sergeant William Ikin who joined the 1/7th Battallion of the Cheshire Regiment and was sent to Gallipoli in August 1915. He got through the campaign, went to Gaza and Palestine but died on 19th October 1917 in a casualty clearing station at Dier El Belah where he is buried.

It was difficult to find information about his army service as the service records of many soldiers were destroyed in WW2 when a German bomb fell on the records office in London. But, piecing together the information that I did have, spurred me on to find out more about that war. I never realised how little I knew of the battles and of these brave men and women who fought in the conflict.

When I began my research, I found the more I read of WW1, the more I wanted to know. And so began a journey that I will never forget.

From the research my brother Stuart Oakes and I wrote a play called Remember Them to commemorate the 100 years of the beginning of the war. Having never done anything like that before we were thrilled when two theatres in the UK wanted to produce the play. In 2014 it was performed and was great success playing to sell out audiences. In 2015 Remember Them won a prestigious award at the Cheshire Theatre Guild. The success of the play spurred me on finish the book. It was very special, unique time for me and I am so very proud to have been part of it.

I want to thank my wonderful friends who have shared this journey with me. They have encouraged me to carry on when doubt crept in, to believe in myself when I questioned my ability, have listened to me relating the story whether they wanted to hear it or not and to Ron Callow for giving me this very poignant title. But most of all my friends have been there throughout. What truly great people they are.

And finally, I want to thank my brother Stuart Oakes. His never ending belief in me, his love and hope for me to achieve my goals and his quiet constant unending enthusiasm has always been there and still is. Thank you Stu for everything.

—

## Sunday 11<sup>th</sup> November 1973

Bill Gibson leaned heavily on the walking stick as he made his way along the cobbled street towards the small terraced house he had lived in for more than half a century. As he hurried along the uneven pavement the damp foggy air snatched his breath; he coughed loudly.

Every Sunday morning he would visit the cemetery on the edge of town and spend time at his wife's grave. On the way back he usually picked up a few groceries from the mini-market on the corner. This Sunday however, after a particularly troubled, sleepless night, he had set out earlier than usual, and had to wait for the mini-market to open. Now he was almost home again. He was ready for a cuppa, to sit quietly and try not to think too much.

Searching his raincoat pocket for his key, Bill heard from afar a sound he knew. A military band was striking up, a regimental sergeant major bellowing the order to march: 'By the left!' Bill stood rigid, listening. Remembrance Day. The annual parade down the High Street, the Mayor and local bigwigs all out looking important in their finest. He had never attended, could never bring himself to –
Bill's hands shook, the key trembling between his fingers as he tried in desperation to get it into the lock. His shopping bag dropped to the ground. Suddenly from around the corner a group of youths appeared.

"Hey it's Billy the drunk!" shouted one of them. The others began laughing.

"What's up Billy boy lost your tongue?" asked the ringleader, "better get a drink down you mate, never too early eh."

"He has it on his cornflakes, too tight to buy a drink down the pub like normal people," sneered one of his companions, a spotty youth with close-cropped hair. From one hand he swung a heavy metal chain.

"Not slurrrring his worrrrddds today," added a third youth, and walked towards Bill in the manner of a drunkard, swaying from side to side. The group joined him, warming to the game, surrounding Bill on the doorstep, pressing their faces close to his, their mocking laughter rising to a shrill cacophony piercing the morning air. The military band had marched out of earshot now, and all that could be heard was the hollow laughter of the boys, a pack of teenage hyenas moving in to strip their prey clean.

—

4

Bill tried the key again, and though his hands were still shaking this time it went in. As he stooped to pick up his shopping bag a booted foot swung out and kicked it over, sending potatoes, carrots and tins rolling across the pavement. His tormentors almost shrieked with delight and began an impromptu game of football with the groceries.

At that moment a window across the street shot up noisily and a woman in curlers put her head out. It was Beattie Phillips, Bill's neighbour. "Hey, clear off you lot, go on get out of it and leave him alone!" The pack stared up at her for a second before the ringleader retorted, "Get back to the zoo grandma!" and picking up a potato he hurled it up at the window.

"I'll call the police!" said Beattie as the potato bounced off the wall and rolled further down the pavement.

"Call 'em, then, we're not scared of no bloody rossers, you ugly old cow!"

"Got an answer for everything haven't you!"

"That's right."

Bill had taken advantage of Beattie's intervention to slip into his house and shut the door behind him. Inside he stood on the mat for a moment, his breathing gradually slowing, his pulse returning to normal. He could hear the youths - jeering, laughing, but then fading away as they carried on along the street.

Peering through the small glass panel in the front door he saw the street was now deserted once more. Gingerly, he stepped outside, waved a brief gesture of thanks at Beattie's window, which was now shut again, gathered up his shopping and returned to the safety of his home.

He made a cup of tea, sat at the kitchen table and glanced at the headlines of yesterday's newspaper; bombs, crime, strike. What a world, he thought. What did we fight the war for?

He had heard plenty of people echo that sentiment, they said it all the time. There had been another war since his, and still people couldn't get on with one another. What had his old friends died for? A country fit for heroes, a better world they had been told. Where was it? Not in this life that was for sure.

Putting his head in his hands he sighed deeply, momentarily unable to move. Those boys bothered him, he feared them, but what could he do? They didn't realise he had been young once, full of energy like them, full of rebellion. But he had respected his elders. It was the way people were brought up then. He would like to be the boys' friend, but they would just laugh at him or worse, probably think he was a pervert or something. Where did it all go wrong for them? Why couldn't they do something constructive with their time? thought Bill, we had the war of course. Always his thoughts came back to the war, like a door that would not close, that kept swinging open, with the endless questions – why, what for, and why am I still here and not in a field in France with my pals. God I miss them.

It was nearly eleven o'clock now but with the fog persisting outside, the house was gloomy. Bill got up and flicked the light switch. Nothing happened. "Damn it," he muttered, "these blasted power cuts, when will they end?"

He found a match and lit what was left of the candle in the brass holder he had been keeping on the table since the strikes began. Soon the wick had burned down and the candle was out, making the room seem even darker after the brief brightness of the flame.

"I will have some light in here." he said again and began searching in the cupboard under the sink for another candle. No joy. Next he went to the cupboard beneath the stairs, the 'glory hole' as Mabel used to call it. Finding nothing there either, Bill returned to the kitchen and began rifling through the drawers, muttering to himself, "I could have sworn there was some candles about..."
He bent down to investigate under the sink more thoroughly, pulling out a miscellany of items; shoe polish, light bulbs, string, screwdrivers, a rusty garden trowel, bits of sandpaper, fuses, nails, tea towels, washing powder, scrubbing brushes, some tarnished brassware.

Soon the cupboard was empty except for a small wooden box lying at the back. Stretching his arm in, Bill hooked the box and dragged it towards him. The box rattled. Bill blew the dust off and opened it. Inside was a half bottle of whisky.

He remembered now, some kind soul at the warehouse had given it to him when he had retired from his part-time job there. "Be lucky Bill," 'he'd said. Nice bloke. It seemed a lifetime ago now. Mabel must have hidden the whisky at some point and it had lain at the back of the cupboard ever since.

He took the bottle out and placed it on the kitchen table. The sound of the band could be heard again. They would be assembling at the war memorial now. He stared at the bottle. The church clock at the end of the street began chiming eleven. The band had stopped, all was still, quiet. Memories flooded into Bill's mind. He picked up the whisky bottle and twisted open the cap.

There was a knock at the back door. Bill put the bottle down and peered though the kitchen window. Beattie Phillips was stood in the back yard.

"Hello Bill, sorry to trouble you love, I saw those lads bothering you again -"

"Oh yes, thanks Beattie."

"Just wanted to make sure you're all right. Do you want me to have a word with Constable Carter?"

"No, no, they're not bad lads really, just -"

"Not bad lads!" Beattie fumed, "they want locking up and throwing away the key – either that or put them in the army."

"I'm not sure that's the answer."

"Teach them a bit of - " Beattie stopped short, staring at the whisky bottle then at Bill. "What's this then?"

"Just looking for candles," Bill replied, his voice trembling. Beattie put her hand on his shoulder and smiled brightly. "You could try opening the curtains properly, and maybe cleaning the windows." She swept the kitchen curtains wide, allowing the weak November sun to filter through the grimy glass. The room looked a little lighter. Without comment Beattie took the whisky bottle and emptied it deftly down the sink. Bill gave a little sigh, the tension leaving his body.

"I'll clean the window with some newspaper and vinegar for you in a bit." She said.

"No, you shouldn't go to any trouble on my account."

"I should, so say no more. And I've got a spare box of candles I'll bring some over if you need them tonight. Lord knows how long this strike's going on for."

"Well perhaps the workers have got a point," murmured Bill, not sounding very convinced.

"Why don't you make a nice fire up in your sitting room, have you got coal?"

"Plenty." As Bill started to walk towards the door his right leg buckled suddenly, causing him to wince, "Ooh!"

"Bill, what is it?"

"A souvenir Beattie, something I brought back from the war. It's alright, just a twinge now and again especially in this damp weather."

"Well take it steady, I'll do the fire."

"No, no, give me something to do, you mash the tea if you like." He set off again for the sitting room, walking slowly.

A few minutes later a fire was burning cheerily in the hearth, and Bill and Beattie were drinking tea. Outside the band had struck up again, the ceremony almost over. Soon they would be marching back up the High Street. Bill was staring into the fire when the rattle of his letterbox made him look up.

"It'll be your Sunday paper I expect, stay there I'll get it."
As Beattie retrieved the paper she opened the front door. Eddie, the paperboy was just mounting his bicycle. "Hello love, didn't mean to startle you," said Beattie, "just having a brew with Mr. Gibson.

"Hello Eddie," called Bill from the sitting room, "thanks son."

"That's all right Mr. Gibson," called back Eddie. He then asked Beattie quietly, "Is he alright?"

"Its those lads again, been up to mischief, upsetting him, and of course its Remembrance Sunday."

"Oh, of course, he feels it a bit doesn't he."

"Yes love, every year, and those good for nothing tearaways are the last thing he needs. I don't know why they can't occupy their time better, I mean look at you, good clean lad, earning a few bob and doing your bit, I don't know. Mr. Gibson's been through a lot, he deserves a bit of respect." Beattie shook her head.

"I know he does. Well tell him I'll see him soon, and don't you worry about those lads, I'll deal with them. They won't be bothering him any more."

"Now you be careful and don't go biting off more than you can chew. They're bigger than you and I wouldn't want you getting hurt. It would be better to speak to Constable Carter."

—

8

"Don't you worry about me Mrs Phillips," smiled Eddie, "I can look after myself, and I've got some good friends too."

"Well don't do anything silly."

"Not a chance, cheerio now."

"Cheerio love."

Beattie shut the front door and took the paper in to Bill. "Here, see if you can find some good news; you never know, the pigs might be flying over today."

For the first time that day Bill smiled. Beattie put some more coal on the fire then made herself comfortable on the settee. Bill opened the paper.

"No sign of the strike ending apparently," he sighed.

"Oh that reminds me," said Beattie, "I must bring those candles over." As Bill lowered his newspaper she gazed at him. "I must say you're looking very smart today,"

"Not bad for an old 'un eh? That's for Mabel, she always liked me in a tie."

"I can see her point. Excuse me being nosey Bill, but are you going on holiday?" She indicated a small suitcase stood in the corner of the room.

"Up to Paul's place, just for a couple of nights,"

"Oh, its today then."

Bill nodded, "To tell the truth Beattie, I'm worried about it."

"Why?"

"He wants me to go and live with him and his family permanently, pack up everything here and move in with them. He says I'll have my own room."

Beattie beamed, "But that's marvellous. I'll miss you of course, but perhaps I can pop up and visit you now and then."

"I'm not so sure...don't put your head above the parapet." Bill gave a short, nervous laugh.

"What do you mean?" asked Beattie.

"The parapet ...in the trenches...that's what we used to say, stay behind it...keeps you safe...don't look over..." Bills expression had clouded, his hands shaking again.

Beattie reached out and put a hand on his arm. "Come on Bill," she said gently but firmly, "this could be a new start for you." She gave his arm a little squeeze.

Bill, breathing heavily, took a sip of tea. "I suppose so, but I've got a lot of memories here...some good.........some bad..."

—

9

"No one can take your memories away from you, you know," said Beattie kindly.

"I'd like to take some of them away." Bill drew in another deep breath. "I've been here over forty years you know. You get set in your ways. It'll be a big wrench just upping sticks and going. Our Paul was a little lad when we moved in."

"And when me and my Alf moved in across the road a few years after, you and Mabel made us feel ever so welcome. We were happy here, same as you and Mabel were."

Bill smiled wryly, "Happy? She put up with a lot from me you know, God rest her soul."

"None of that was your fault Bill," said Beattie. "It was the war that did that." She patted his arm reassuringly. "Me and Mabel had many a chat you know, she understood you more than you realised."

"I put her through it Beattie," Bill said sorrowfully, "I put her through it, the nightmares, the dreadful dreams. I couldn't stop them."

"She understood, and I'm sure Paul does now. Why do you think he wants you to go and live with him? Bill, don't feel guilty, you weren't a well man. That's over and done, in the past, and your son obviously accepts that. I tell you what, let's see if there's anything you've forgotten. Have you packed your pyjamas?" She got up and opened the suitcase and checked the contents.

"Never argue with a woman," said Bill, and going to the fireplace he took down his pipe and tapped it on the side of the fire grate, sending the ash into the flames. He removed the lid of the wooden jar that stood on the mantelpiece, filled the pipe with fresh tobacco and lit it. "There's some things that never leave you Beattie, no matter how hard you try, they never go. I came back with some terrible memories, but them sort of memories you don't share."

Beattie closed the suitcase and came over and stood by him. Taking his hand in hers she said softly, "Oh Bill, can't you let it go? This isn't like you, you were doing so well."

"I've never done well, that's the point."

"Look, you don't have to go to your son's you know, not if you don't want to."

Bill drew on his pipe. "That's just it Beattie, I do. I'm lucky, some people haven't got a soul in the world, but I've got a wonderful son, and a good friend in you."

"Right spoilt aren't you!"

"The chance to get to know him again is a gift, unbelievable, but he still feels like a stranger to me. The fact that he came back after all these years to find me, I can't let it go I know; I've got to make an effort. But I should have done it when Mabel was here, that's the trouble, that would have made everyone happy."

Beattie looked thoughtful for a moment. "We all have regrets Bill, but we can't turn the clock back."

"Don't I know it!"

"Now don't go all sad on me Bill, not today. The saddest words in the English language are what might have been. You know what I think?"

"What?"

"That Mabel's looking down now, and that her heart is overflowing with joy to know that you and her beloved Paul are reconciled again."

"You really believe that?"

"That there's an afterlife, that we go on? Certainly I do. I couldn't carry on if I didn't. And I think you believe that too, in your heart of hearts. It's what takes you to that cemetery every Sunday without fail, rain or shine, week in week out, all year round."

There was a long silence as Bill gazed into the fire. It was as if he were searching deep in the caverns of flame for something, something beyond words, searching for meaning, for an ultimate answer to the greatest riddle of all, the mystery of life and death. After what seemed an age he said, "Do you know it's three long months and two even longer weeks since I had a drink?"

"And you've done very well. That's why I poured that bottle of Scotch away. You don't hold it against me do you?"

Bill sighed, "No, you did the right thing. But have I done well Beattie? What if you hadn't come in when you did? Would I have opened that bottle and drank the lot? Course I would, I'm a drunk, whether I'm drinking or not, I always was and always will be, that's why those kids take the mickey, I don't deserve anything else. Maybe their fathers are as useless as I was. I was certainly no father to Paul, gave no thought for him or his mother. I was safe with the bottle you see, safe from the torments. The more I drank the more they stayed away…until the next night. No wonder Paul left home, he couldn't take any more of my rambling, my self pity, and I let him go Beattie."

Bill slumped into the armchair and sank his head in his hands. "It's the ghosts you see Beattie, people laugh but it's the ghosts."

"I'm not laughing."

"It's the lads, they won't leave me, they're there all the time lately, I don't know what to do."

Beattie sat on the arm of the chair. "Maybe if you talked about the things that happened, talked about your friends, the ones that never made it, maybe that's what they want you to do. And I think they would be listening too, just like Mabel is."

Bill lifted his head, his eyes suddenly glowing with emotion, "You know Beattie, maybe you're right, maybe that is what they want." He stared again into the amber glow of the fire. "I remember it like it was yesterday, the birds singing, the sunlight on the dew, that beautiful September morning in 1914."

# CHAPTER ONE

September 1914

Bill Gibson flicked the reins gently across the backs of the two carthorses as they trod the rich, loamy earth.

"Come on Bess, get on Dolly," he said kindly "A couple more hours while we've got the light, then we're done."
The animals quickened their pace, Bill guiding the heavy wooden plough behind them. He loved being in the company of these great majestic creatures. The tide of recent events had made him realise just how much they meant to him in every sense.

The war that had been raging in France and Belgium for some weeks now was claiming not only human lives; the British Army, desperate for cavalry mounts and transport for munitions and heavy artillery, had been requisitioning horses the length and breadth of the land. Many of the neighbouring farms had already given up their animals. Bill had breathed a sigh of relief that his employer Mr Haughton had kept Bess and Dolly. The horses snorted and dipped their huge heads as if agreeing with his thoughts.

Suddenly Bill heard his name being called. "Whoa girls, whoa." He pulled on the reins and Bess and Dolly halted obediently. Looking across the field he saw Albert Tomlinson waving as he clambered over the stile.

"Where's the fire Bert?" he laughed as his friend ran towards him.

"Bill!" panted his friend.

"Don't tell me the pub's run out of beer."

"No chance – but it might do tomorrow - them Army men are back."
Bill frowned, "I know, I saw the poster same as you, they're recruiting in the village hall tomorrow, well they won't be seeing me there."

"Why not?" asked Albert, "Me and Tommy and Harold are thinking of going."

"Good luck to you, I mean it." said Bill as he gathered up the reins

"It's a good life in the army Bill, better than sticking around here where nothing ever happens."

Bill looked out across the sweeping landscape with its folded hills, the meadows dotted with sheep and the farm cottages nestled into the valley. He took off his cap and scratched his head.

"Oh there's a lot happens here Bert," he said thoughtfully, "first the sun rises, then you have a cup of tea and bite to eat. You go to work, and you sweat and your arms get tired. Then the sun goes down and you come home, or you might go for a bike ride or help Dad in the garden before your supper."

Bert threw back his head and laughed, "You're a right stick in the mud Bill. Have you no sense of adventure?"

"No, I'm quite happy to stay here, and work on the farm. You have a good job too Bert, We don't need anything else."

"But they'll be time enough for that when we come back. The farm will still be there, the factory won't shut and they'll still be here when the battles are done, and so will England."

"I don't doubt that Bert, with brave lads like you to fight for her."

Bert was serious now, "Don't you want to be one of them?"

Bill shook his head." Who'll plough the fields and bring in the crops?" He shook the reins; the horses slowly began to move forward. Albert grabbed his arm.

"The women and the old men, you're only seventeen same as me, we've got our whole lives ahead of us."

"Well maybe I'm an old man at heart."

"Maybe you are. And I don't mean you're no coward when I say that."

"I know. I wish you luck."

"Well, I'd better get going Bill." Bert turned to walk back towards the farmhouse. A few yards on he stopped and called back, "Oh Bill – I meant to say, they're after horses too."

"They can ask all they like because Mr Haughton's not giving up Bess and Dolly, he said so."

"Thing is, this time they're not asking – they've given out a requisition order."

"They've made a mistake then, because Bess and Dolly are needed for agricultural work, Mr Haughton told them. He's already written to our MP about it, and our MP's an important man. So you go and tell them War Department wallahs where they can stick their requisition orders. I answer to Mr Haughton, not the bloody army."

# CHAPTER TWO

Kitcheners Volunteer Army

The crowd in the village hall had swelled to some forty people by the time Albert arrived. He nodded to his friends Tommy, Harold, and Jacko who were sitting in the front row of chairs waiting eagerly for the proceedings to begin.

"Bert – down here," called Harold, "we saved you a seat!"

"Eh, you've no business saving seats," remonstrated a middle-aged woman sat in the row behind, "besides you're all young enough to stand."

"We will be standing soon enough Mrs Ikin," replied Tommy, "we're joining up. Is that what you're here for?" He winked at Harold and the pair exchanged a snigger.

"My William is already a soldier of the King I'll thank you to know," sniffed Mrs Ikin.

"You signing on with him then are you?" said Harold archly, "make sure he gets his bacon the way he likes it and tuck him up in bed of a night?"

"Don't you be cheeky with me young man – my William's giving a talk today about life in the army, and you'd do well to pay attention if you know what's good for you."

Tommy nudged Harold, "Oh yeah – I hear they made him General – did you hear that Tom? General Willie Ikin – and him all of 19 would you believe!"

Harold turned to Bert who had now joined them and said, "Is Bill coming?"

"Nah," said Bert, "Too busy with his horses."

"He'll regret it, doesn't know what he's missing – while we're off having adventures and thrashing the Hun he'll still be ploughing that blessed field."

"Till kingdom come, or till the cows come home!" Jacko scoffed.

"And the horses" Tommy grinned. " And talking of cows - do you think old Ma Ikin here's is our new secret weapon?"

"She'd give the Kaiser a run for his money all right!" Jacko laughed

"Hey, hey, that's enough of it you lot, don't you go giving Mrs Ikin none of your sauce now, if you're going to be soldiers you should know better and mind your manners."

Tommy and Harold looked round at the strong, broad shouldered figure of Gabriel Plunkett the village blacksmith.

"Sorry Mr Plunkett," said Tommy, deferential now, "but I was only saving a seat for Bert, so as he doesn't miss a chance of joining up."

"All right," nodded Gabriel sternly, "but that's no excuse to not show some respect for elderly people, like Mrs Ikin here."

"Elderly people - how dare you?" said Mrs Ikin indignantly, "I'd have you know I'm a darn sight younger than you Gabriel Plunkett!"

"Sorry dear, I meant elders, elder people, see I was only -" protested Gabriel.

"Don't you damn well 'dear' me!"

"Language Mrs Ikin, language," murmured Tommy mischievously.

"A bit of hush if you please ladies and gentlemen!"

On the stage a uniformed NCO with an impressive bristling moustache was calling the meeting to order. He rapped his knuckles on a wooden table set beneath the proscenium arch and the heavy velvet curtains, the proud possession of the Village Players swished open. Revealed were three soldiers in smart khaki uniforms stood to attention and gazing out at the assembled company. A smattering of the Players who happened to be in the hall instinctively applauded prompting everyone else to join. A little boy at the back called excitedly, "Mummy, the show is starting!" the remark greeted with indulgent laughter and further clapping.

"Those lads look the part eh," whispered Bert to his friends. "I'll reckon they don't go short on girls."

"Neither will we soon as we get togged out," grinned Jacko. A voice from the wings bellowed the command "STAND AT EASE!" and as in unison the three men stood easy, an even more immaculately dressed soldier marched on, a junior officer in khaki peaked cap and jacket, beige jodhpurs and glistening brown leather boots.

Taking centre stage he tapped a swagger stick in his leather gloved hand and surveyed his audience.

"Thank you for coming here today," he began. "My name is Captain Andrew Stubbs. As you all know the war has now been in progress for several weeks, and -"

"You call it progress?" interrupted Maurice Cole the village postmaster.

"I do sir," replied Stubbs

"Your lot say it'll be over by Christmas, so will it?"

"My lot – and who pray is my lot?"

"You know who – politicians, officers, them what's supposed to be in charge, supposed to know what they're doing – not sending our lads like lambs to the slaughter."

Mutterings of agreement arose from some sections of the audience. Stubbs stood his ground and let the noise subside of its own accord before continuing.

"I understand your concerns. War is not pretty and neither is it simple or predictable. It is true there have been losses, but nothing worthwhile is possible without some sacrifice. What I can assure you all is that we have right on our side, and that we will win this conflict and ensure the continued freedom of Britain and her empire. Yes many people, myself included, hope that it will be over by Christmas. I for one cannot deny that I want that to be so. The tide is now turning, and it is turning in our favour. What I say to the young men here is, join us now in fighting for your country, and you will come home heroes."

Captain Stubbs paused and studied the faces of the people before him. Some looked sceptical, others bemused. Many were visibly stirred. A lone voice called out, "Hear, hear!" followed by silence.

"Private Jabez Hulse," ordered Stubbs, "step forward."
The middle soldier took one pace towards the front of the stage.

"Hulse has just returned from the front. He is as well qualified as any to tell you all what it's like there."

Taking a deep breath, the young private shifted from one foot to another.

"Well, first of all, talking to you lot's more terrifying than the Huns I can tell you straight off."

This seemed to do the trick. Several people laughed, and an immediate lifting of tension was felt throughout the room.

"Go on Jabey, spit it out pal," called Tommy Fisher, "you don't usually have any trouble." The laughter grew louder.

"Ah but that's when I've had a drink or two Tom," said Hulse bashfully. He turned to his superior, "Sorry sir, I'm a bit nervous."

Stubbs smiled, "Carry on Hulse," he said in an undertone, "just a few lines, as we rehearsed - it's going well on the front line, food's good, French girls etc."

Hulse nodded and turned back to the audience. "It's going well on the front line, we're pushing back the German army and gaining ground. The food's good, and the French girls bring us loaves-"

"Bet that ain't all!" called out Bert.

There was more laughter, whistling, and some disapproving looks from the women in the room.

Hulse, now visibly trembling attempted to continue but before he could utter another word Mrs Ikin piped up, "What about my Will? He was told he'd get to say his piece. So when will that be?"

"And so he shall madam," assured Stubbs. "Come along then Ikin, make your mother proud and tell us all what you've been doing for King and Country."

William Ikin stepped forward beside Hulse and cleared his throat. "Next month I am about to leave for France, to the front line, my turn to do business with the Hun."

From the crowd came cheers and shouts of jubilation and encouragement. William Ikin raised his hand, and when his audience had quietened he carried on.

"As I said, I'm off to France, I've never been on a boat before, never been to a foreign land and yes I'm scared, scared of what we might find, scared of what's waiting for us, but I'm prepared to face it, me and a good many others who feel the same way as I do." He waited again for the crowd's approving response to subside.

"Some of us..." the young man hesitated, a faint tremor now in his voice which he struggled to control. "Some of us," he began again, "will not come home."

This time the audience did not cheer but lowered their heads, murmuring softly and nodding respectfully, while the faces of some tried to mask their fear and apprehension as the implications of the speaker's words sank in. Ikin, fighting his own inner demon, in a bid to subdue it raised his voice several decibels.

"But when all the battles have been won," he shouted, punching the air with his fist, "and this damn war is over, some – many of us - will come back, back to our homes and lives and families, knowing that what we fought for was right and true. And those we leave behind - will be forever honoured!"

For a second there was a spell binding silence in the hall, followed by the most thunderous burst of applause and cheering yet. Ikin, visibly flushed and sweating now broke into a half relieved, half embarrassed smile of appreciation. "So I am - um - looking forward, yes very much looking forward to getting to grips with the Hun - " There was more cheering – "and of course, will be pleased to accept the kind gifts of many grateful French womenfolk."

The gravity with which the young soldier delivered this last remark produced outpourings of mirth much as a pompous fool in an over earnest tragedy might bring comic relief to its emotionally exhausted audience.

Stubbs called order. "All right everyone settle down. Now we'll move on to the purpose of today's meeting, and what I know several of you young lads are waiting for. So, do you want to be soldiers? - I said -do you want to be soldiers!"

A cheer went up from Tommy, Bert, Jacko and Harold, and a dozen other young men now present at the back. Stubbs nodded to a colleague waiting at the piano who struck up a rousing chorus of *'Soldiers of the King'*

"Well come along then, Sergeant Prosser," ordered Stubbs, "get those forms ready."

The four lads at the front rose to their feet as those at the back pushed their way forward to the accompaniment of much cheering, clapping and hearty slaps on the back. Making their way onto the stage amid the tumult Bert turned to Tommy. "Here you don't suppose that's true what old man Cole said do you - about lambs to the slaughter and all that?"

Tommy shook his head, "You know old Coley, he's never one to look on the bright side, never even steps out of doors when its raining, I reckon he's just jealous he's too old to join up."

19

Bert laughed, "Yeah, you're probably right there. Now I just wish I could persuade Bill to come with us."

"Just a minute" a voice rang out from the crowd. "Who's going to look after my wife and kids if I don't come back." Stanley Jenkins strode forward and looked the captain in the face. "I said, who's going to look after them," repeated Stan.

Captain Stubbs adjusted his cap, pulled his jacket straight and spoke in a clear, concise tone. "Provision has been made for families, individual circumstances will be considered." He held Stan's stare for a moment then turned his attention back to the throng, "Now come on lads, sign up please, come and fight for your king and country!"

His appeal was quickly answered as the young men cheered again and more pushed towards the stage. Stan moved aside and stared at the lengthening queue of youths, all full of high-spirited humour. His expression was grim; only that morning he had seen soldiers no older than these coming up, being taken into the nearby cottage hospital. Some had lost legs or arms, some bandaged around the face, hiding what hideous wounds he dared not imagine. Perhaps, he thought mordantly, those who did not return were the luckier ones. He gazed at the poster on the wall, at Kitchener's mesmerising finger, extended it seemed directly at him.

### KITCHENER"S VOLUNTEER ARMY
### YOUR COUNTRY NEEDS YOU!
### ENLIST TODAY.

"You joining 'em then Stan?" Gabriel Plunkett nudged his shoulder.
Stan frowned, "Don't know what to do Gabriel. The country's calling for us, I'm for saying let it call, and not rush into the ranks as this lot are. Where's the justice in it?"

"Ah, Stanley, I daresay you have a point, I've seen this mess coming a long while now." said Gabriel sagely.
Stanley nodded in agreement. "Aye, so have I. So have I."

"Then why are you thinking of going, Stan." Gabriel asked. "Let them young 'uns go. We did our bit in Africa."

"I know mate" Stanley replied, "But she needs all the help we can give her."

"Then let them that's got the riches they want to cling on to do the fighting." Gabriel uttered. "I owe this country nothing, neither do you."

"I know what you're saying is right. Why should I risk my life to fight for god knows what. Them in their posh houses don't help me. I live in a slum, work all the hours God sends and get paid a pittance and I should be grateful to them - can 'ardly make ends meet." Stan said bitterly, "But on the other hand - if I takes the kings shilling like they're offering – well, it's more than I get paid now, Lil will be able to feed the little "uns."

"Look out mate, here's your missus." Gabriel nodded towards the door, "And she don't look happy."

"There you are Stan," said Lily Jenkins crossly, "I've been looking everywhere for you, I thought you said you weren't interested in these sorts of goings on?"

Cradled in her arms was their youngest daughter Phoebe, just one year old. Lily's swollen midriff heralded their next arrival, due any day now.

"Where's Jonno and Reg?" asked Stan. These were their two young sons, seven and five years old.

"With my mother, I had to come and find you Stan, I was worried - you shouldn't be here."

"Neither should you in your condition," Stan nodded towards her bulge.

"I'm alright," replied Lily in a matter of fact tone, "it's when they're here you feel done in."

"And four mouths to feed then, as well as thee and me."

"We'll manage."

"Will we?" said Stan. "You know the army pay good money Lil, a lot more than I earn, and it'll be all yours. I'm not ending up in the workhouse like my grandfather."

He turned towards the stage, the cheerful banter as each young man signed his name while the piano played on, ringing in his ears. "If the government would look after you and the little ones, why even I might go and face them Germans. But then what if I get knocked out, busted up. Oh, what the "ell, what the "ell -" He tailed off lamely and shook his head, wracked with painful indecision.

Lily handed her daughter to a woman stood nearby. "You saw them wounded lads," she hissed at her husband. "You want to end up like them? Some hero you'll be, looking like that!"

21

"That's no way to speak Lil."

"I speak as I find."

"The pay would be handy love,"

"Damn the pay, I say. Forget this joining up lark Stanley Jenkins, we need you, not money, nor this blasted war. Let them fight as want to, you're too old besides, you'd be no use to them anyway."

Stan shook his head again and sighed heavily. "I don't know. I'm thinking now there's no use keep talking about it. Those poor lads up the hospital, and I'm sitting it out here without a scratch on me - I couldn't look "em in the face, Lil"

"What of it?"

"I'm going."

"No, you're not."

"I'll tell 'em I'm under forty-one, and face the music come what may with our boys out there. I've made up me mind."

Lily's face contorted in anger and distress, "You're a fool Stanley Jenkins," she screeched, "a bloody fool!"

Several heads turned and stared at the couple now.

Stan shrugged. "Maybe you're right Lil, but I'll have no peace of mind if I stay here. I'm weary of trying to convince myself otherwise, I've got to go Lil." Kissing her on the cheek, he turned, made his way towards the stage, and a few moments later had signed his name.

All the formalities were completed, and the nine young men who had enlisted stood in a slightly self-conscious huddle at the front of the hall. A cheer went up, as the door at the far end opened and Edwin and Winifred Barnett, proprietors of the Nags Head appeared wheeling two large trolleys laden with drinks and sandwiches.

"It's on us everyone," announced Edwin, "but our brave lads first eh!"

"'Cor! Thanks Mr Barnett," said Bert appreciatively as he was handed a glass of ale.

"You can call me Edwin," beamed the landlord, "after all you're a man now eh!"

"And you know what to call me!" Feeling a hand on his elbow Bert turned. It was young Emma Cole, the postmaster's daughter.

---

She gazed at Bert in undisguised adoration. "You're going to look even more handsome in that khaki. Just don't forget about me waiting back home for you when those French girls come out with their cakes eh?" Drawing him aside she lowered her voice and continued, "And don't take any notice of what my stupid father said – lambs and slaughter, what nonsense trying to frighten young men from the call of duty! I'd have a good mind to give him this only it's for someone else."

Looking down Bert saw in her hand a white feather.

"Oh, Emma, um, what do you mean?"

"Bill Gibson! The lily livered good-for-nothing weakling, should be ashamed of himself skulking on that farm with his precious horses while you lads are stepping up to do what's right."

"Well I daresay Bill has his own reasons Emma."

"Only one reason – it's called cowardice -"

"Someone mention my name."

Emma and Bert turned to see Bill Gibson.

"Well, if the cap fits," said Emma coolly.

"Bill, good to see you," said Bert awkwardly, "we've joined up like we said we would, me and Tommy, Harold, and Jacko. ...-"

"But you're not old enough none of us are and Jacko, well, he's just a lad not more than fifteen."

Bert shrugged, "Well, we've joined up now and that's that, Come and have a glass of beer with us."

"No thanks Bert, I won't." said Bill.

"I should think not," said Emma tartly. "But you're quite safe now, the recruiting officer has finished for today. This is for you by the way." Taking his hand she pressed the white feather into it. Bill held it aloft.

Realizing what was happening the hall had gone silent and everyone was now looking at him. Breathing hard, Bill shoved the feather back at Emma. "You were right Bert," he said.

"About what?"

"They're taking Dolly and Bess in the morning, there's nothing we could do, not even Mr Haughton."

"Oh – I'm sorry -"

"Don't worry Billy boy," purred Emma, "I'm sure you'll get some more little gee-gees to play with while Bert and his friends are hundreds of miles away fighting for our country."

At this there was a sharp intake of breath around the room. But Bill appeared not to have even heard the remark. Instead he looked at his friend and said, "Bert, would you ask the recruiting sergeant to kindly open his book again."

Albert looked puzzled. "Why do you want him to do that?" He asked

"I'm coming with you." Bill replied.

A resounding cheer filled the village hall. The pianist responded to the jubilation and hammered the keys once more to an even louder encore of "Soldiers of the King."

Meanwhile, Ernie Fowles the village newspaper seller, having stood by himself throughout the noisy proceedings and observed all that had gone on, opened the door and slipped quietly away.

Some half an hour later, the hall was empty. A young soldier entered and climbed the steps to the stage. In the silence of the room Jabez Hulse gazed at the poster still hanging above.

Softly, as if in a dream, he began to speak to an invisible audience.

"I once believed the lies, just as the fools who signed their names here today have done. Yes, I've just come back from the front. That was about the only truthful thing I said. To say it's a hellhole out there doesn't begin to describe it. But I too have spun the lie. I should now go and find them and confess that I spoke such terrible lies. I recognise their enthusiasm, but I also know their fate.

When I first saw this poster on the railway station wall, it inspired me. Only now I see men that wrote it. The hands of fat civilians, I bet they're thanking the Almighty they're too old to follow its oh so noble call. We who have been there know what the poster ought to say: Come and lay down your life so the King can sit peacefully on his throne. But don't expect a quick death, not unless you are very, very lucky. Come to hell on a one-way ticket.

We'll call you a hero, call you anything you like if you'll just jump when we say jump, perish when we say perish. You might even have a few moments, hours or even days of excitement, of pride, thinking what a great brave fellow you are, and how fine you must look to the ladies and the millions of dullards back home with brains stuffed full of complacency and deceit who actually think there's something worth fighting for in this lunacy and bloodletting and insane murderous nonsense. Gallantry, sacrifice, patriotism, comradeship – fill your ears with enough of that horse swill, and whatever agony is coming your way might even seem a little less awful for a brief second. That's what I'd tell them." the young man muttered bitterly to the empty air, "Those brave and beautiful, idiotic recruits. If only I had an ounce of courage left in the miserable bag of untruth and confusion I used to call my honour I'd…."

At that moment hearing a noise behind him he broke off his monologue and spun round. Coming from behind the heavy red curtains was Gabriel Plunkett.

"Oh -" stammered Jabez awkwardly, "I thought I left my gloves here."

Gabriel nodded but said nothing as the young man walked quickly past him and out of the building. Gabriel, who had returned to lock up, had been standing there for several minutes. Looking up at the recruiting poster now he said quietly,

"Well I could never have put it as eloquently as that young man, Mr Kitchener, sir, but truth to tell, there's a part of me that could willingly carve every word he spoke just now into your arrogant heart."

Taking the key from his pocket Gabriel closed and locked the door, leaving Lord Kitchener staring silently in the empty and darkening hall.

That night, up at the stables, a lantern glowed softly. In among the hay Bill stroked Dolly and Bess in turn, feeling the warmth of their strong gentle bodies. As they each responded by nuzzling affectionately against him, the young man closed his eyes against the falling tears.

# CHAPTER THREE

Fond Farewells

"Oh Billy I've never seen you look so fine, you're like something out of a picture book!"

Elsie Gibson, bursting with all the pride that is the prerogative of a sister seeing her much loved younger sibling in uniform, straightened his collar and brushed non-existent dust from his tunic.

"Six weeks training and you've gone from a boy to a man." She sighed and squeezed his arm affectionately, "But to me you'll always be my little brother, that mischievous mite that used to tease the cat and spill his milk on the floor."

Bill pushed her hands away and readjusted the collar. "Stop it Elsie, it was all right as it was."

Elsie persisted, "All grown up, but forever a little boy at heart, still needs a woman's touch."

Hearing the conversation, Mrs Gibson called from the kitchen, "Elsie, stop your tormenting and set the table, Bill wants a good meal in him, 'fore he goes, not a lot of fussing."

"No," winked Elsie, "he'll get enough of that from you on the doorstep I'll warrant." She took a clean white cloth from the dresser and slapped it playfully at her brother's head, She then laid the cloth on the table, neatly smoothing the corners while Bill put out cutlery for four. The clock above the fireplace began to chime noon.

Bill stopped and stared at it. Two more hours, he thought, and I'll be walking down to the station, and tomorrow morning boarding a boat for France. Looking around the familiar room, the only home he had ever known, the idea of leaving England's shores, let alone going off to war seemed utterly unreal.

Mrs Gibson emerged from the kitchen bearing a steaming earthenware dish and set it down on the mat in the middle of the table.

"Fetch the carrots Elsie, oh and the butter. Billy get the bread - and sit down, your father will be here any minute."

The click of the latch on the back door announced the arrival of Mr Gibson senior.

"Hello, hello!" He shouted cheerfully.

"Hello" Mother son and daughter replied in unison.

After hanging his cap and jacket on the hook behind the door and washing his hands he strode into the front room, where their smiling faces greeted him.

"Hello, Hello all," he said again

"Sit down dear," said Mrs Gibson, "This will be the last meal we have with Bill…" she paused. "Well – for a little while…pass up your plate James." She ladled out the stew and handed it back to him. "

"That's a good smell Mags," he said as his wife handed him the plate.

"We can thank our Billy for that." Mrs Gibson smiled proudly across the table at her son.

"Mr Haughton gave me a basketful of provisions for us all," said Bill.

"Now let us please say grace," said Mrs Gibson." The family closed their eyes obediently in prayer. "For what we are about to receive may the Lord make us truly grateful. Amen."
Bill tore off a hunk of crusty bread and dipped it into the rich gravy. "Yeah, Mr Haughton wished me well, said my job would be waiting when I come back."

"Well that was kind of him Bill," beamed Mr Gibson. "You want to keep him to that."

"Though when that'll be I for one can't say." murmured Bill. "After all, in time of war who knows what will be."
Hearing her son say this a shadow fell over Mrs Gibson's countenance, "Now let's have none of that talk Billy." There was a noticeable tremor in her voice.

Mr Gibson coughed awkwardly while Elsie spoke up in an attempt to allay her mother's fears, "All he's saying is there's no knowing how long this business might go on for – they said it will be over by Christmas"

"Which Christmas?" Mr Gibson chortled through a mouthful of stewing steak.

"But the Kaiser will get what's coming to him sooner or later," continued Elsie.

"You're right there girl," agreed Mr Gibson heartily, "and with Bill and his pals on the job now, I'll warrant it'll be sooner, eh lad?" He slapped his son vigorously on the back.

"He should have a job to come back to, it's only right," said Elsie, "because he'll be a hero will my little brother!" She reached over and pinched his cheek teasingly.

Bill looked thoughtful. "I don't know about that," he demurred.

"What do you mean?" said Elsie.

"Well, the way I see it, the real heroes are people like Sid Murray from Willow Tree Farm."

"True lad," Mr Gibson bowed his head solemnly. "And Georgie Frost the herdsman, God rest his soul."

"The heroes who never came home," said Bill in a faraway voice.

The atmosphere round the table had turned chilly. Seeing her mother on the verge of tears Elsie, putting on her brightest voice said, "All the more reason to be proud of our Billy for doing his bit, and honouring what Georgie and Sid did."

Mrs Gibson laid down her cutlery. "And what did they do?" she said querulously, "not yet 21 years old, and left their poor mothers grieving - "

"I thought you'd be proud to see our Bill serving his country," said her husband.

"Oh I am, of course I am," she insisted, her voice still shaking, "it's just that now the moment has come I'm – oh - only a mother would understand."

"And, perhaps a father," put in Mr Gibson. Seeing his wife's eyes brimming with tears he reached over and gently squeezed her hand, "Now, now love, don't take on like that, not on Bill's last day."

The unfortunate choice of words was too much for Mrs Gibson, and with a wail and a flurry of skirts she rose from the table and ran sobbing to the kitchen.

"Go see to her Elsie," said Mr Gibson.

"I'm sorry Dad," said Bill, "I didn't mean to be gloomy, or to upset ma."

"I know lad."

"It's just that I think about things, you know."

"Too much thinking is not always a good idea son."

"Perhaps you're right."

"All you need to know is that we're proud of you, and we've every respect for your decision to enlist. If I said I wasn't going to worry about you as much as your mother will, then I'd be a liar, but us men have our own ways of saying things."

"I spoke unwisely."

"And I know that brave as you are, you'll have worries of your own, any man who's not a fool would. But I know that along with courage you've a good head on your shoulders, and that when the cannons are shouting you'll know when's the right time for valour, and when to follow the better part of it and keep your head down – for your own sake and that of your comrades. Am I right?"

"You're not often wrong Dad, and I know you'd be going too if you could."

"What man wouldn't? You'd make any woman proud son. Oh and on that subject, that young Emma Cole was asking about you while you was away training."

"Emma?"

"They do say she's always been sweet on you."

"At one time maybe Dad, but after what happened at the recruitment day it doesn't look that way any more."

"The white feather you mean? I heard about that too."

"Here, you don't think that's why I joined up do you, to try and show some stupid girl I wasn't afraid?"

"No, no, I know it was the horses going that made your mind up."

"As a matter of fact it wasn't."

"No? What then, the thought of Sid and Georgie and all the other lads that'll never come home?"

"Them yes, but there's also the lads who have come home, but will never be the same again. It was Stan who made me think of it."

"The blacksmith's labourer you mean? I heard he'd enlisted, though he must have lied about his age, he's well past forty years old. Fit as a fiddle and strong as an ox mind you, hands the size of shovels and just as hard, I pity any Fritzy who gets in his way!"

"I bumped into him in the village on the day of the recruitment," said Bill, "told me where he was going, and the reason why."

"Oh?"

"Yeah, told me he'd seen some boys in khaki back from the front, in the back of a lorry going to that big old house they've turned into an hospital. He said some of them were in a real bad way - no legs, no arms. Said he was ashamed to look them in the face. 'So I'm going,' he says to me, 'and I'll take no argument about it.'"

His father nodded, "That sounds like Stan all right."

"So Dad, my joining up has got naught to do with any girl." He then sighed heavily, "And anyway Emma was all over Bert that night."

"Surest sign she's still sweet on you."

"How do you figure that out?"

"Women are canny that way, but once you learn to read them you'll do all right. Making eyes at another Fella is a woman's way of telling you she's keen on you. She's a fine looking girl son, and though I say it myself she'd be lucky to land a fine chap like your self. She'd make a good wife and all."

"But the white feather, it seemed such a cruel thing to do in front of everyone-"

"She's still a girl, and girls do foolish things. Everyone in that hall knew that, and they've always known you're no coward, and now you've proved it. Hell hath no fury like a woman scorned lad – Emma must have got the idea you was ignoring her, and her passion got the better of her and made her do a stupid spiteful thing, something she barely knows the meaning of. Chances are she's now regretting it and wants to make amends. Ah, the course of true love never did run sweet."

Bill frowned, "Hmm, I don't know about love, you're confusing me Dad – and if Bert thinks she's got eyes for him, he's not going to thank me for chasing her."

Mr Gibson tapped his nose sagely, "Let her do the chasing son, and as for Bert, he's big enough to look after himself."

"Well I still don't know – I did always like Emma but...I'll have to give that one some thought."

"But not too much eh? Remember what I said, too much thinking sometimes gets you nowhere. Well that's my bit of fatherly advice for today, and anyhow, before you or Bert or any of you can think about courting, you've got a war to win."

"Just the five of us eh?" laughed Bill.

"If you can stay off the beer long enough, I know what army life can do to you lot when you get together."

"There'll be no beer for us Dad, you know that,"

"You're in the army now son, there'll be beer shouldn't wonder."

"We'll be lucky to see the inside of a pub where we're going."

"All the more reason to lick the Kaiser and get back here double-quick then isn't it!" Mr Gibson gave his son another firm slap between the shoulder blades. "Now come on and eat up, here comes your mother, there's nothing cheers a woman up like seeing her men-folk eat a good dinner – providing she's the one 'as cooked it of course!"

This made Bill laugh out loud just as his mother and Elsie returned to the table.

"Oh I'm glad you're going off in good spirits son," said Mrs Gibson still dabbing at her eyes with her handkerchief, "you are in good spirits aren't you Bill?"

Bill smiled, "Hearts of oak ma," he proclaimed, "that's what we Englishmen have."

"You never spoke a truer word my boy," said Mr Gibson.

"Ma, forgive my pessimism earlier," said Bill, "it was just the wish to remember Sid and Georgie at this time, and give them their proper due."

"They'll get that on high too lad," said Mr Gibson echoing the sentiment, "St Peter won't have asked no questions when those two brave lads turned up at the Pearly Gates, straight on to glory -"

"Pa…" Elsie kicked her father's foot under the table and nodded in the direction of her mother.

Mr Gibson did another of his coughs, "But what we're concerned with is life down here on earth and keeping everything going in their memory, and what have you, -"

"Here, here!" cheered Elsie clapping her hands.

There was a knock at the door. Mrs Gibson went to answer it and ushered in a rubicund middle-aged lady, dressed in muddy farm overalls.

"Aunt Bertha!" cried Bill and Elsie at once.

"Hello children," she said beaming fondly at her niece and nephew.

"It's a long time since these two have been children Bertha," Mr Gibson laughed. "Especially this strapping young man in uniform here."

"I know, but they'll always be children to me," replied Bertha wistfully. "I've brought this for you Billy." She handed Bill a small shiny object. "A lucky cat," she explained, "keep him safe and he'll look after you."

Bill turned the object over in his hand for a moment; "It's so small, I might lose it, you keep him safe for me Auntie, and give it to me when I come back." He dropped it into her hand.

"I will do that Billy," she said; then proffered her cheek for his customary kiss.

"The good Lord will be watching over him too, don't you worry Bertha," assured Mr Gibson.

"He watches over all of us dear," said Aunt Bertha, and placed her hands on her sister shoulders.

When it was time to go, Mr and Mrs Gibson, Elsie and Aunt Bertha came to the garden gate with Bill. Albert Tomlinson was already there, waiting for his friend and now, comrade in arms.

Bill couldn't help smiling momentarily at the sight of his family lined up in such stiff regimental fashion to see him off. Elsie was first to hug her brother, followed by Aunt Bertha, then Mr Gibson. Finally came his mother, enfolding him in her arms and not wanting to let him go, till her husband gently eased her aside and held her back. Albert picked up Bill's kit bag. Bill smiled and took it from him. Both of them turned towards the lane leading from the cottage.

The family stood, watching from the little slip of garden. As the young men reached the bend at the top of the small incline they turned and gave one last wave.

## Sunday 11th November 1973

"It was a strange, lonely feeling walking away and leaving my mum and dad there at the gate," said Bill. "Unsettling. I'd never been off the farm or away from my family before. I felt proud though, felt like a real man, but I think now that was a false feeling. With every step I took, looking back and seeing my parents dwindling in the distance, every now and then there was this awful hollow feeling in the pit of my stomach. Unconsciously, there was that little grain of concern - would I see them again? It nagged away at me, quietly, but it was always there at the back of my mind. We all felt the same. I know Albert did, and Tommy, they told me so later on. I suppose it was the realisation all of us come to at some point, war or no war."

"That one day our parents aren't going to be there?" said Beattie.

"Yes. I think my fear was that they might die while I was away. Odd wasn't it? I wasn't so worried about myself, not at that stage anyway."

Seeing the painful look that had come over Bill's face, Beattie smiled to reassure him. She then said, "And did you miss Emma?"

Bill managed a smile in return, "Emma was never my girl or was ever going to be - she was Bert's. And even if she was sweet on me I wasn't sweet on her." The painful expression returned to his face, "And then of course she gave me that white feather."

"That was a wicked thing for her to do Bill," said Beattie.

Bill sighed, his mind grappling, trying to come to terms with the event that almost sixty years ago had hurt him so. "Well, she'd read in the papers what them women were doing in London. I dare say she thought it was the right thing to do. There were plenty that agreed with her."

"Well she should have been ashamed of herself, that's all I can say."

Bill's expression changed again, his train of thought focusing hard, "But what she did Beattie, *was* the real reason I signed up that day, not what I told my Father. I didn't want to go and that's a fact, the euphoria of that moment didn't excite me like it did the others."

"No?"

Bill shook his head, "It had just the opposite effect. But I didn't want to be thought a coward, that would have been a terrible thing."

"You were never that Bill,"

"I was afraid to be seen as afraid, if that makes sense, afraid of the shame, which would have reflected on my family too. But I had yet to learn that at some point in that war Beattie, we all did cowardly things."

For a moment, there was an awkward silence between them, Beattie wanting to say something but not sure what would be right. Then taking another long draw of his pipe Bill continued.

"As I said, I'd never been away from our village until then, none of us had. When I could forget worrying about my mum and dad, about what might happen to them, the trip abroad was a big adventure, like a holiday you could say, especially as they had told us the war would be over soon.

The train station was full of soldiers, new recruits boarding for the south coast. Most of them were laughing, joking - all good lads. Being amongst them I stopped missing my family. Those lads were such fun: you couldn't imagine anything bad happening when you were with them, and as the train got going I really started enjoying myself. We stopped at several stations and more soldiers got on, all fired up and cracking more jokes. Before we knew it we were at the training camp, row upon row of white tents, field after field as far as the eye could see. It was as comfortable as could be expected.

There were a few of us to each tent and we all had a camp bed, not what you could call luxury but we weren't sleeping on the ground."

"You made do," said Beattie.

"Exactly. And we were young don't forget, and most of us were used to the outdoor life, we'd grown up that way. You know, we still thought of it as a holiday when the sergeant, a fierce creature with a foghorn of a voice told us in no uncertain terms that it wasn't! We just smirked at one another when he wasn't looking. We were there for months - weeks of marching, training, day after day learning to shoot our Lee Enfield rifles, how to throw grenades. How to kill."

"And did it begin to sink in then?" asked Beattie, "the real reason the army wanted you there?"

Bill's expression darkened. "They hung sacks from a wooden frame and we had to run at them with our rifles, bayonets fixed, while this gruesome sergeant shouted "Stab them in the heart lads! Think of those sacks as Germans. It's you or them!" Geeing us up, shouting the same thing over and over, to try and give us the killer instinct I suppose. So we'd run at these sacks, yelling at the tops of our voices and shove our bayonets in, turning them, twisting them so as the stuffing would fall out on the grass."

"A stupid question," said Beattie, "but how did that make you feel?"

"No it's not a stupid question," said Bill, "we just got on with it I suppose. It did begin to seem less like a holiday then. With that monster of a sergeant bawling at us we just did what we were told. You could see some blokes really enjoying it, like kids playing a spiteful game or something – the Sarge loved them! Me, I was just glad to make a hole in the sack and keep the so and so off my back."

"What about those that didn't do so well?"

Bill shook his head. "There was hell to pay for anyone that wasn't up to the mark. They never called it bullying - instilling discipline, that was it. I suppose the NCOs had a job to do getting us lot into shape but some of them were cruel, no feeling for another man's suffering whatsoever, and if they took a dislike to you, it was God help you. I remember one lad, Arthur Quigley. He was only eighteen a big, awkward, clumsy lump, but strong as an ox with it. He had a hell of a time of it. He couldn't shoot in a straight line, nor throw a mortar or even stab that sack. He was so ham-fisted; we even had to help him load his gun, much to the sergeant's disgust. That sergeant had it in for Arthur that's for sure, threatening him, bullying him, goading him, relentless he was. The poor sod was scared to death, couldn't get it right. I don't know how he stuck it, even I felt like lamping that sergeant for him."

"I don't blame you!" said Beattie.

"Then one morning the sergeant being his usual bombastic self began to pick on Arthur again. This particular day, I remember it had been raining, the ground was awash with mud but that was no excuse to stop the training. The Sarge was in a particularly bad mood and of course Arthur copped it. This made the poor lad worse, kept dropping his rifle and stumbling in the mud. The sergeant laid into him good and proper till eventually Arthur broke down, dropped to his knees with exhaustion and couldn't go on."

"Poor man," said Beattie, "what happened then?"

"It was so unexpected. The sergeant marched over to Arthur reading him the riot act, leaned over and punched him hard in the ribs."

Beattie winced, "The bloody sod! Oh, excuse my language Bill."

"We said much worse," Bill grinned, "under our breath, of course. But now came the unexpected bit - as the sergeant swung his fist to hit him again Arthur got to his feet, grabbed the man's arm and twisted it. Then we heard something snap."

"You don't mean - he broke his arm?" gasped Beattie.

Bill nodded. "That great bully fell to the ground screaming in agony. Arthur just stood there, staring."

"He couldn't believe what he had done probably," remarked Beattie, picturing the dramatic scene Bill had described.

"I think you're right. Anyway the other NCOs were on Arthur like a flash. Someone blew a whistle and a few minutes later the military police were taking him off."

"And what happened to him?" asked Beattie.

A faraway look came into Bill's eyes. "None of us ever found out. There were rumours he'd been sent to prison for a few months and was let out with a dishonourable discharge. But we never saw him again."

"That sergeant deserved what he got by the sounds of it."

"I agree," said Bill. "It was just a shame that a nice gentle bloke like Arthur was driven to do what he did. After that, things seemed a bit more lenient in the training camp. We got a new sergeant, a decent sort, bit more amiable, as far as an NCO could ever be. We got a bit of time off too, away from camp." Bill laughed, "We had some fun, all of us lads together, found our way to the local village pub, met some girls, all innocent but it lifted our spirits. After all the square bashing and getting shouted at, I felt life was worth living again."

Beattie laughed, "You Bill, enjoying yourself, well I never did."

Bill smiled, "You can laugh, but I wasn't always an old codger."

"Didn't say you were."

"I've had my moments Beattie. The uniforms did the trick with the girls just like Albert said they would. And of course there was the drink -" Bill stopped mid sentence his mood suddenly altered as he sat staring into the past, lost for a moment in time.

"Anyway, after a few more weeks of training, marching and discipline we were ready to leave. Now we were soldiers, ready to fight. The time had come for us to board the ships for France. No more fighting straw sacks. We were to meet the enemy, and get a taste of what that war was all about."

"Were you excited, nervous?" asked Beattie.

"Bit of both I suppose; in that short space of time Beattie we'd gone from innocent young lads to strong confident men ready for whatever the Germans were going to throw at us. Well, that was the idea at least. We couldn't be beaten, and the powers that be, well, they'd assured us that it would all be over within a few months...."

# CHAPTER FOUR

Folkestone England
February 1915

Amid a chorus of honking horns and shouting NCOs, the snaking line of canvas clad trucks pushed its way through milling cars, bicycles and civilians, and pulled in along the esplanade that topped the high cliffs overlooking the English Channel.

On the command from their officer "All out!" the tailgates fell away the young soldiers piled out. Bert, Bill, Tommy, Harold and Jacko quickly formed a lively huddle, along with two other new recruits, Charlie Ingles and Jimmy Benyon whom they had befriended on the journey down from the training camp.

"Wake up and smell that Bert!" said Jacko.

Bert rubbed his nose and sniffed. "What is it?"

"See that great dollop of water out there?" Jacko took his friend by the shoulder and pointed towards the sparkling ocean spread out below them as far as the eye could see. "It's called the sea."

As the others laughed Bert momentary paused, "Blimey – I've never seen the sea before."

Jacko drew in a deep breath "Clears your lungs does that,"

"So does a fag," said Tommy, "I'm gasping."

"Me an' all, have one of these." Harold tossed him a cigarette. "Anyone else – Charlie?"

"Thanks mate." As the cigarettes were lit Bert asked, "Have you seen the sea before then Jacko?"

Jacko hesitated, "Well erm…. not in so many words like."

"Either you have or you haven't."

"Me Auntie Winn sent us a postcard from Blackpool once – that had a lot of sea on it." There was more laughter.

"Anyone else?" Bert said.

The young men murmured awkwardly and shook their heads.

Charlie Ingles lowered his kit bag onto the pavement and sat on it. The smoke wafted round them in the breeze and they were quiet for a moment lost in their own thoughts. Charlie took a photograph from his breast pocket and gazed longingly at it. Albert leaned over.

"She'll wait for you Charlie, don't worry," he said patting the young man's shoulder.

"Yeah," said Charlie, "yeah, course she will, not worried about that."

"What's her name?" Bill asked peering over his other shoulder.

"Edith."

"You going to marry her?"

"I already have."

"Oh - how long have you known her? Harold asked.

"Three months."

"That's a bit hasty isn't it?"

Charlie frowned. "Do you think so?"

"Not up the duff is she mate?" asked Jacko.

"Jacko, mind your manners," chided Tommy. "Take no notice of him mate."

"That's all right," said Charlie, "and no she's not as it goes. We both wanted to get married though, before I left."

"She looks a very nice girl Charlie, you done the right thing putting a ring on her finger." said Tommy.

"Yeah," agreed Jacko, "the ring will make other chaps think twice about taking liberties while you're away."

"Oh lord, you don't think they'd try that do you?" Charlie had gone pale.

"Jacko why do you have to say the wrong thing every time you open your mouth?" sighed Harold. "All he means is Charlie, that ring tells the whole world the girl's yours and no one else's."

"Mind you," continued Jacko obtusely, "some lads consider a married woman that much more attractive, a bit of a challenge -"

"Where did you meet her mate?" interrupted Harold loudly, while frowning sternly at Jacko to be silent.

"In the tobacconists."

"Cor strike a light!" quipped Jacko.

"Shush, let the man tell his story."

"Yeah, let him speak," said the others.

"Well Jimmy and me had called in the shop for some baccy, there was a bit of a queue and I was about to leave. Then I saw her, stood behind the counter. She had a smile for every customer and I wanted her to smile at me, such a lovely smile it was, like an angel, I couldn't take my eyes off her. Then when I finally got to the counter, she was staring at me with her big blue eyes, smiling with those beautiful red lips, close enough for me to reach out and touch her, well -"

"Well what?" chorused the listeners.

"I forgot what it was I wanted."

"Yeah the cat got his tongue good and proper," Jimmy Benyon slapped his friend's back and laughed. "The silly sod just stood there helpless. So I stepped in."

"What, you asked her to walk out?" said Bert.

"Yeah, but not with me, with him, I was Cupid," said Jimmy proudly.

"And thanks to him she said yes," smiled Charlie.

"And if she hadn't, I would have taken her out myself straightaway," added Jimmy.

"I thought you were supposed to be Cupid?" said Harold censoriously.

"Cupid ain't stupid," grinned Jacko.

"Only joking," said Jimmy, "anyway I could tell from the way she was giving Charlie the come on, it was him she liked."

"Let's hope it stays that way," said Charlie looking slightly worried again.

"Don't you fret mate, it sounds like love at first sight," assured Harold.

"Or first light, seeing it was a tobacconists."

"Will you belt up Jacko? A tobacconists shop is as romantic a place as any – it was obviously a match made in heaven, and seeing Charlie I can imagine her eyes lighting up over the counter as he – oh for goodness sake…."

The whole group fell about laughing at Harold's unintended puns, drowning out his words. "A match made in heaven! Lighting up over the counter - here Bert, hear that?" Jacko called to Bert, who was still leaning by the esplanade wall staring in wonder at the ocean.

At that moment Sergeant Prosser strutted into their midst. "Come on look lively you lot! Pick up your kit and fall in at the double!"

The young men broke off their conversation and shouldered their kit bags. "That includes you Tomlinson!" barked Prosser at Bert.

"Sorry sir, yes sir." Bert turned and fumbled with his gear. "Look lively there!"

"It's the first time he's seen the sea Sarge," volunteered Harold, helping Bert on with his kit bag.

"First time for all of us Sarge," said Tommy.

"Jacko's seen it on a postcard, but that was Blackpool -"

"Well that there's the English Channel," snarled the sergeant major, "and if you lot don't look sharp you'll be swimming it, all twenty two bloody miles."

A blast from the ships' hooters resounded around the bay, followed by a renewed volley of bawling commands from the other NCOs.

"Fall in there at the double, in line, four abreast, fall in!"
With a clatter of boots several hundred soldiers stumbled rapidly to attention, shoulders back, heads held high, and row upon row of khaki uniforms formed up along the cobbled road. Sergeant Prosser paced up and down.

"Where are we going Sarge?" Jimmy asked.

"Down to the beach for a nice day out lad," snapped Prosser, "got your bucket and spade?"

"Eh? Oh yeah, ha-ha."

"But first we've got to make a little detour to France, a training camp, and then off to the front line."

"Front line?" said Jimmy anxiously, "thought we'd be heading for Belgium Sarge, to help out like?"

"Oh we'll be helping out all right," said Prosser grimly. "Don't you worry about that. No more questions, and smarten up you lot, you're in the British Army now serving King and Country, and we don't want to let them down do we - WHAT DON'T WE WANT TO DO?"

"Let them down Sarge!" replied the young men in cheerful unison.

"That's more like it, right look lively now, and no talking in the ranks; here comes your marching orders."

41

A senior NCO at the head of the line bellowed, "Attention!" Several hundred pairs of boots clattered together. "By the left…march!"

Uniformed limbs swinging in time, the long column of men moved smartly off down the winding slope towards the harbour, the cobbles rattling under their feet, while the crying gulls wheeled and circled above. Their sergeant major now out of earshot, Charlie said to Bill, "She isn't up the duff you know."

"We believe you mate, honest."

"But in a way I wish she was."

"Why would you want that now?"

"Keep the toe rags away," said Jacko.

"No, because he loves her," corrected Bert. "The same way I love Emma."

"How do you know Emma wants you though?" said Bill.
Bert shot Charlie a sideways look and the two of them grinned. "Some things you just know, Bert laughed. "You'll understand the ways of women one of these days Bill."
Bill made no reply.

"Plenty of time for that when we get back," piped up Jacko, "Me, I'm in no hurry, besides I'm not interested in love, and not sure I want to understand them. I just want to get a look at these French girls we've heard so much about, or are they Belgian?"

"We're headed for France the Sarge reckons," said Jimmy from the row in front.

"French, Belgian, what's the difference," chuckled Jacko, his eyes twinkling, "they're all foreign, and you know what they say about foreign girls don't you?"

Any reply was lost in further blasts from the ships" hooters, much louder now as the column of men drew closer.

"All right all right," said Tommy with a smile, "leave off your blooming trumpet salty, what's the hurry?

"If I have to tell you miserable lot once more about talking in the ranks," glowered Sergeant Prosser reappearing at their side, "I'll have the lot of you chained to a gun carriage in no man's land as target practice for the Kaiser - is that clear!"

The boys immediately fell silent and continued their rhythmic marching, descending the last few hundred yards to the harbour. Moments later they had arrived on the quay and from the front of the column came the command "Stand at…ease!"

---

"Well there they are," said Harold nodding towards the two large troopships stood at anchor, gangplanks lowered and their crews busy about the decks.

"I've always wondered what it's like going on a big boat," said Bert nervously.

"Jacko will tell you, he's probably got a postcard," said Harold.

"I'll shove it up your Khyber in a minute," retorted Jacko.

"Only joking Jacko, never call it a boat though,'cos that's what goes down a river, the sailors don't like it called a boat, it's a ship see." Harold lowered his kitbag, opened it and took out his packet of cigarettes. As he did so however, without warning there was a flurry of renewed activity ahead, and the column of men appeared to have begun moving towards the ships.

"Oh, looks like this is it lads."

Sticking his unlit cigarette between his lips, he shouldered his kit again and got hastily in step with his fellows, the quay now a mass of shuffling khaki.

As the five friends drew closer to the water an NCO held out his arm. "You five carry on, the rest of you to the right."

Harold, Bert, Bill Tommy and Jacko were the last to join the nearer ship, now apparently full, while Charlie and Jimmy were the first to board the other.

"Lucky blighters," Harold called out to them across the swaying gangplanks, "you'll get the pick of the seats. Send us a postcard Jimmy!"

"Send one yourself - see you in France Harold!"

When all decks were crammed with men and the anchor ropes gathered, there came a final blasting of hooters and the two steel leviathans began to move slowly off from the quayside. As the local townsfolk gathered on the esplanade they took off their hats and waved. The sound of cheering broke out along the ships' railings. It began uncertainly, then slowly swelled to a resounding and glorious triumphant roar of comradeship, a rallying battle cry of belief. The young men feeling all the excitement of a great adventure now waved at the crowd. A spirit of uncertain readiness for whatever might be was now in their minds.

As Bill looked out from the stern he noticed that a third ship had set out from further along the harbour and was now following in their wake. He felt a sudden pang of distress on seeing that the vessel carried not men but horses, in what looked like huge numbers tethered uncomfortably close together on the decks. He turned his eyes away in anguish, thinking of his own Dolly and Bess. He prayed that the twenty- two miles of the English Channel would soon be crossed, and that all the animals would soon be safely on dry land.

A mile out the surface of the water began to change, a heavy swell appeared and the ships began to roll and lurch. At first the soldiers greeted this phenomenon like a joyful fairground ride, laughing and whooping as they collided with one another and struggled to stay upright. Then after a while the humour drained away, and some men began to look distinctly uncomfortable, pushing their way to the railings to be ill. On the first ship, Harold rallied his friends with words of advice,

"Not to worry lads, we'll soon be ashore and getting a nice hot brew of tea. Look at the horizon, that's the trick I believe, that way your head fooled your stomach, or something like that."

Bill Gibson smiled at his friends reassuring words. He took one final look back at the receding shoreline. Would we ever see it again? He thought. The realisation was beginning to hit home.

This journey, this adventure was turning into something different, something very real. Were they taking a trip of a lifetime, or were they lambs to the slaughter.

# CHAPTER FIVE

France
1st March 1915

There was audible relief on the decks of the two troop ships as the gangplanks clattered down. The disembarkation got underway and a few moments later Bill Gibson, Tommy Fisher, Harold Braithwaite, Jacko Wilks and Albert Tomlinson stood together for the first time in their lives on foreign soil. The glad relief to be off the pitching sea and on terra firma once more had given way to a more subdued mood, a sense of not knowing quite what to expect next. Tommy sat down heavily on his kitbag.

"Thank God that's over," he sighed. "Don't think I've got anything left to bring up."

"You do look a funny colour mate," Albert said offering him a cigarette.

Tommy, still a little green around the gills, grimaced and shook his head, "No ta, don't fancy one yet." He squinted across at the little fishing village that lay beyond the stone jetty, then along the rugged French coastline, miles of empty beach stretching as far as the eye could see on either side, the only sign of habitation an occasional cottage or two. Although coming up to midday the sky was lead grey and ominous. "Not exactly Blackpool sands is it?" he remarked.

"Well we're not on holiday mate," said Harold. "We've a job to do, and when we've done it we can get back to Blighty and celebrate."

"Or Blackpool," grinned Tommy."

"Wherever you like mate."

From among the throng a voice rang out, "Right let's be moving and sharp about it!"

"Hey up," said Harold, "no peace for the wicked."

Hundreds of pairs of boots began tramping over the cobbles towards a line of waiting trucks, and within a few minutes the British contingent was winding its way across the French countryside.

The pale light was fading further when the first of the trucks turned in at a gate. Bill, Tommy, Harold, Jacko and Albert peered out at a muddy field.

"Where are we?" asked Tommy.

"The middle of bloody nowhere," said Harold.

"See any French girls?"

"Only the four legged kind." Harold pointed to a herd of cows grazing by a copse of trees. "Won't hurt you."

"The pong might spoil your chances with the mademoiselles, they prefer eau de cologne," grinned Albert.

"Come on look lively you lot!" Sergeant Prosser was banging the tailgates of the trucks and chivvying the men towards a row of huts on the far side of the field.

"That our billets?" enquired Tommy. "Could have dropped us right outside, save us walking through this mud."

"That's the whole point lad," said Prosser, "don't want the vehicles getting bogged down, besides they're due back at the coast to pick up another detachment from Blighty."

"Popular this party ain't it?" quipped Tommy.

"Yeah, very glad I booked a ticket in advance," agreed Harold as the five friends joined the trail of soldiers trudging their way across to the huts.

"Here listen," said Jacko, "they're having a sing-song."
Sure enough, as they came closer to the billets, a low chorus of male voices could be heard in the breeze.

"Oh…the…mademoiselle from Armentieres, parlez-vous, the mademoiselle from Armentieres, parlez-vous, the mademoiselle from Armentieres, hasn't been kissed in forty years, hinky, dinky parlez-vous…"

Rounding the corner of the huts, Tommy, Harold, Albert, Jacko and Bill found a group of soldiers with their uniforms unbuttoned and hats off sat around a smoky fire, mess tins of tea in their hands. Their singing, though the words were risqué had a melancholy air about it.
Tommy raised his arm in cheerful greeting, "Hey lads, mind if we join you?"

The singing stopped as the men looked up at the newcomers. None of them spoke for a moment then one man, unsmiling muttered in a broad Scots accent, "Just got off the ship I take it? Well, welcome to hell laddie."

Tommy laughed uneasily. Another of the seated group then said, "That ain't no way to greet a rookie Jock, not on his first day."

"Better that than kid him he's come for a fortnight's jolly."

"We know that mate," said Harold heartily. "We're here to do our bit just like you blokes, show the Hun what for and send him back where he belongs."

At this the Scotsman and his comrades laughed quietly and mirthlessly to one another. He then extended his hand towards the ground.

"Take a soft tuft of grass or a log if ye can find one, and be seated. We're all friends here. Then we'll put ye wise on a thing or two"

The boys shook hands with the veterans, gratefully accepted offers of tea and sat themselves down.

"So how are things going out here?" said Tommy brightly, "we've heard there's a big push coming."

"Tell me now, in which direction would that be?" said Jock. This time the laughter was more fulsome.

"Yeah, want to get that right I suppose," said Tommy laughing along with them.
Jock's face then took on a more serious expression as he leaned in towards the fire. "The word is," he said quietly, "they're going to try."

At that moment there came a sudden loud noise over their heads.

"Christ almighty!" yelled Albert diving face down onto the ground. His four friends likewise cowered, Tommy crossing himself fearfully.

"Ha, ha, ha!" Jock and the others were laughing uproariously. "Ye needn't worry lads, that was only the Royal Flying Corps saying hello." The bi-plane that had skimmed the field was already a distant speck in the sky.
Tommy, his cheeks smeared with mud sat up, "You mean to say that was one of ours – what the bloody hell were they trying to do – kill us?"

"Bloody show-offs the RFC – but if it was the Red Baron we'd know all about it by now."

"What were you saying before Jock?" said Albert brushing the mud from his battledress.

"Aye, well its strictly hush-hush, but there's rumour of an assault being planned on the enemy line over at Neuve Chappell."

"Neuve who?" said Tommy nervously, still not quite recovered from the surprise of the RFC's low flying antics.

"'Tis only a little village I understand," said Jock, "but riddled with Germans."

"Dug in up to their top knots," added another veteran, "a mile of barbed wire, razor sharp, and machine guns every fifty yards."

Albert shivered. "Haven't we got machine guns though?"

"Not like theirs," said a third veteran.

"The British Army has not as many overall, they say," qualified Jock.

"Well, we'll have rifles," said Jacko

"A machine's worth fifty rifles," said the second veteran.

"A hundred more like," countered his comrade.

Jock raised his hand to adjudicate, "Estimates vary, the firepower might be equivalent to maybe eighty of our Enfield's"."

Tommy gave a low whistle, "Crikey."

"Surely they're not so accurate?" said Bill

"They don't need to be," said Jock grimly. "They have the effect of a scatter gun, hitting a man in open ground is like hitting a barn door."

There was silence for a moment as the recruits contemplated this stark description. Then Tommy piped up, "Ah but our artillery boys can knock out their machine guns before we go in."

"That's the theory," said Jock in a non-committal tone.

"How do our big guns know where to aim for though Jock?" asked Albert. "If the Bosch are well dug in I mean?"

Jock jerked his thumb skywards to where the plane had flown a few moments ago. "That's what yon flying boys were doing today I'll be bound."

"A reccie you mean?" said Harold, "find out exactly where the Bosch are, and what they've got?"

Jock nodded then said, "Watch out, this looks like your Sergeant."

Prosser marched up, "When you lot have finished swilling tea and having your mother's meeting, there's some rifles round the back with your names on."

Though the new recruits had all received a few days of basic weapons drill back at their British training camp, insufficient rifles had been available for issue at the time. Tommy and Albert looked both thrilled and apprehensive now at the prospect of finally receiving their own rifles.

"Hope I can remember what we learned on the drill," said Albert anxiously as they left the camaraderie of the campfire and went to line up at the munitions store behind the billets.

"Piece of cake," said Harold reassuringly. "Just make sure to point the sharp end away from you before you pull the trigger."

Each man was issued with a Lee Enfield 303 rifle; the recruits then followed their NCOs making their way to their billets. Pausing at the corner of one of the huts, Harold pointed to a pair of large bell tents painted with the Red Cross insignia. "Looks like they've got a makeshift hospital here as well," he observed. He turned to his friends, "Tell you what, let's go and have a word with some of the wounded lads, see if we can cheer them up a bit eh."
Tommy looked dubious, "Oh, I don't know Harold."

"Frightened of a drop of blood? Think how they feel. Come on, they might be glad of a chat." He led the way over to the tents. As they approached a piercing scream rent the air. "You know, I don't think they'll want us getting in the way," said Tommy anxiously.

At that moment the tailgate of a truck that had just arrived rattled down. Two uniformed nurses appeared from one the tents and hurried over. "Don't just stand there staring," said one of them, "lend a hand here."

"Right, yes ma-am," said Harold quickly, "happy to oblige."
The four friends joined the nurses at the back of the truck, helping down the injured men. All had field dressings to various parts of their bodies, several had missing limbs, and the heads of four were almost completely swathed. Tommy and Albert took hold of one of them.

"Careful, careful there!" admonished one of the nurses, a stern matronly woman, "haven't you been told how to carry an injured man? You could make things worse." Bustling over she readjusted the position of their arms around the soldier, "that's better, take him in, slowly does it, the doctors will tell you where to put him."

49

The tent flap opened and a doctor, shirtsleeves rolled up and braces hanging loose barred their way. "I've no more room in here you chaps, you'll have to sit these fellows outside till we can get a couple more tents rigged up -" He was interrupted by another scream from within. "Give him more morphine," he shouted over his shoulder, then to Tommy and Albert, "jump to it then."

The wounded were quickly offloaded, laid on stretchers under the elements, or sat up against packing cases.

"Smoke pal?" Harold said to a man with bandaged eyes.
The man nodded.

"What's it like out there mate?" asked Tommy.
The soldier wearily lifted his head. "Hell on earth," he answered, his voice hollow, "It's Hell."
Tommy and Harold, looked at each other, then Harold spoke. "So, what's it like in the trenches?"
The other soldiers now lifted his head. "Horrible" he whispered, "The cold, mud, lice, the rats. What more do you need to know?"

"Here pal have your smoke," interrupted Harold.

"Is it night?" asked the first soldier. "Why is it so dark?"
Harold pressed a cigarette in his hand and said hesitantly, "No, not quite."

"Am I blind?"
Harold said hesitantly, "No, no - you've had a rough time that's all, but you'll be back to Blightly now, they'll get you fixed up, you'll be on the mend soon enough."

As Harold lit his cigarette for him, the man gave a kind of brief sob, "Sorry, sorry -"

"No need to be sorry," Harold patted his shoulder, "you've done your bit now it's our turn; we'll give the Bosch a good hiding for you mate don't worry."
The man began shaking now, and chanted repeatedly, "What's the sense in it, what's the sense in it."

"Come on Harold," whispered Tommy, "let's leave these blokes in peace. We're going to need some rest, like you say, we'll be doing our bit soon enough."

Harold lit a cigarette and took a long hard draw on it. "He's right you know, what *is* the sense in all this. Those poor sods, maimed, wounded, it doesn't seem right."

---

"Come on mate, don't take on so, they'll be alright, off home to blightly and the sooner we get through this then we'll be going home. Just think there'll be a big celebration for us."

"That's all very well, we might end up like them lads or even worse. There but for the grace of God, Tommo."

"Oh cheer up Harold, you worry too much we'll be alright, just stick together. Anyway, we've got a dance to go to tonight. With a face like that you'll scare off the ladies."

"If your Maggie knew you were looking for a bit of skirt she'd sort you out."

Tommy laughed, "I'm not, she's the only one for me and I'm going to marry her when this is all over. We're going to have lots of kids and a nice place to live. What about you?"

Harold shook his head, "There's no one for me; I've not met anyone I fancied yet."

"Then tonight's the night, mate" Tommy heartily slapped Harold back, "The girl of your dreams is waiting at the dance, just for you."

In the distance they heard the low rumblings, felt the earth gently tremble beneath their feet.

Tommy looked at the sky, "Thunder; must be a storm coming; looks like rain."

Harold looked up at the sky, "There's no storm coming Tommy, that's not thunder, it's coming from the front line and in a couple of days that's where we'll be."

# CHAPTER SIX

Love and Rivalry
8th March 1915

By 7.30 the next morning the camp was already bustling with life. Having slept through reveille, it was the clatter of equipment, accompanied by a hubbub of voices that summoned young Bill Gibson to consciousness. Emerging sleepy-eyed from his first night under canvas, he gazed out at the row of identical white tents stretched across the field. Beside each one, soldiers were busily marshalling themselves and gathering their mess tins as their NCOs barked orders. An aroma of cooking wafted from the direction of the huts. Bill poked his head back into the tent, "Eh, come on lads, hurry up or we'll miss breakfast."

A series of groans was swiftly followed by a flurry of activity, and a few moments later Harold, Albert and Tommy stumbled into the daylight, joined from the adjacent tent by Jacko, still buttoning his uniform. "Guess who's in my tent." he said
Albert shook his head,

"Jabez Hulse, he turned up late last night, didn't say much just dropped onto his bed and fell asleep."
They pushed through the tent flap.

"Jabey!" Albert said, shaking him awake. "Nice to see you mate, thought you were going somewhere else."
Jabez yawned and slowly sat up. "We were until orders came down that half the battalion was going over to Egypt, Bill Ikin's gone over there, going to be a big push rumour has it, fighting them Turks in a place called Gallipoli. Wish I'd have gone with him; they'll have an easy time of it, lucky sods."

"Yeah, but you're with us now," Tommy said, slapping him firmly on his naked shoulder. "Come on, get up we're going for some breakfast."
Jabez grabbed Tommy's arm and slapped him back, "Get off me you big gawp." He said, "I'm not hungry, now if you would kindly leave me alone." He grabbed the covers and turned his back on them.

"Lets go," Albert, said, "He's a grumpy old sod"

"Bring your mess tins," said Bill leading the way out of the tent, "Don't know about you lot but I'm starving -"

"Get out of the way!" came a loud shout as a laden cart pulled by two horses went thundering past.

Bill jumped aside just in time. "Thanks," he said panting with relief at the near miss.

"You want to watch out pal," The young soldier who had cried out the warning was Jock whom they had met the day before. "Yon wagon lads are nay fussy who gets in their way, bit crazy if you ask me."

"He wants to watch out too," rejoined Bill, "driving horses like that, he's liable to do them an injury."

Jock laughed, "This is war pal, they can't be fussed about dumb animals."

"Dumb animals, how dare you talk like that," said Bill vehemently, "Horses are God's creatures same as you and me."

"Take it easy," said Jock looking quite nonplussed, "save your fighting spirit for the Bosch, you're going to need it. And just remember, if the rations run out we'll be eating horses, so don't get too sentimental about them."

"How can you say such a thing?" demanded Bill.

"The Frenchies eat them all the time, tis a rare delicacy. Take your pick between horse and rat, I know what I'd rather have, not much meat on a rodent."

Bill, not knowing what to say to this, stared in distress at the other man. Harold took his arm and steered him away. "Come on Bill, don't let's let him put us off our breakfast."

On leaving the canteen hut later however, the two men found themselves side by side. "I meant no offence earlier on. I take it you have a fondness for horses. I shouldn't have made light of the matter. You're right, they don't always get treated as well as they should, and after all they never volunteered to come and get shot at did they?"

Bill looked at him, "You've changed your tune," he said.

"It was a rotten tune. Ma pals always tell me ma mouth's bigger than ma brain! But I was worried for you when I saw that wagon coming."

"Oh, that's all right," said Bill. "And thanks again for what you did, I'd have been mincemeat under that cart if you hadn't shouted. I can see I'm also going to have to toughen up a bit out here. I'm Bill Gibson, and yes I do work with horses, grown up with them, and they mean a lot to me - my two were taken by the army."

"Don't worry," said Jock, "you'll have taught them good sense, and if they're in the cavalry they'll be well cared for."

"I hope so." Bill said thoughtfully. "Have you been here long?"

"About a week, top brass are getting us ready for the big push so I hear. Going to the concert tonight?"

"Concert?"

"A few of the nurses are putting on a show here in the canteen, some of the lads do a turn and all, bit of singing and dancing, you know." Archie said encouragingly, "Come along pal, could be a long haul before we're back in Blighty, enjoy yourself while you can. Probably be a drop of French plonk too."
Bill smiled, "Sounds good. I'll think about it."

"And bring your pals, there'll be plenty of nurses to go around, they're bringing a new lot in tonight, fresh from Blighty – a girl for every bloke they reckon!"

"Thanks, I'll tell them, - even if I don't come."

That evening the canteen quickly began to fill. A long day of drilling and getting shouted at had left most of the men in sore need of some relaxation. Bill however had, for reasons he could not quite fathom himself, not felt in the mood. The idea of meeting girls filled him with excitement, but also trepidation in equal measure. He knew that even if he so much as danced or held hands with a young woman, he would feel awkward, as it would be the first time he had been in the company of a young woman at close quarters. In the end Albert had persuaded him to come to the concert.

"Why did you want to come Albert?" he asked as they went in and found space on a wooden bench. "Didn't think this sort of thing was your cup of tea?"

"It's a woman," Harold said, appearing next to them and cuffing Albert's ear playfully. "One of the nurses."
Albert looked sheepish. "Nah, nothing like that," he muttered, "It's the plonk I'm here for."

"You've never drunk plonk in your life," joshed Harold.

54

"All right, all right," conceded Albert, "I was only passing the time of day with her."

"So that's what they call it now!" came a gleeful chorus from Tommy and Jacko who had just arrived.

Harold nudged Albert excitedly, "Look mate, look there she is." He nodded towards an attractive, dark haired young woman who had just entered the canteen. Several dozen pairs of soldiers" eyes watched as she took a seat on the small rostrum set up at the far end.

"What's her name Albert?" whispered Tommy.

"Camelina Rodriguez."

Tommy and Jacko snorted with laughter.

"Pack it in you lot," said Albert, "that's what she said her name was all right, I think she's Spanish."

"What's she doing here then?"

"She's a nurse of course, what do you think she's doing?" Albert was quite exasperated by now.

"All right, all right, calm down, " said Harold, "eh up, what's Jabez doing?"

Jabez Hulse had approached Camelina on the rostrum and was leaning over, appearing to be talking intimately with her.

"He's got a nerve," said Albert, "what's his game?"

"Probably just passing the time of day with her, same as you were," said Harold. "It's a free country."

"Whose side are you on?" said Albert.

"No one's, and there's plenty more fish in the sea – here what about that nice brunette just come in."

"I fancy her," said Jacko.

"She'd eat you for breakfast." Harold laughed.

At that moment the band, which consisted of the M.O on a battered upright piano, his chief orderly on double bass and a jovial looking warrant officer with a fiddle, struck up energetically with the tune to "Soldiers of the King."

"Oh not this again," groaned Harold, "can't they play summat a bit more lively?"

"You'll be looking lively in a minute," rasped Sergeant Prosser, "When I march you off to a court ruddy martial, now sing up! Oh We're Soldiers of the King We Are…"

"Who invited him?" lamented Harold shaking his head as Prosser strode along the benches, urging all and sundry to "Sing Up!"

A moment later the musicians began to play a slow waltz. "Take your partners please," announced the M.O.

The soldiers needed no second bidding and were soon escorting the young nurses onto the somewhat rickety wooden floor of the canteen. Albert however was incensed that Jabez Hulse had beaten him to Camelina, and refusing to ask any other girl, he sat stubbornly through the first dance with a bitter and envious look on his face.

Then as the music drew to a close Harold urged him to take his chance.

Albert took his cue, "Here, budge over Jabey, I'm next."

Jabez smiled at him with cold courtesy, "I was here first, isn't that right Miss?" Camelina inclined her head graciously her dark curls falling over sultry eyes. Albert, obliged to withdraw, found himself locked in the next dance with an earnest young nurse with wide eyes who stared at him in rapture for the entire time, much to the amusement of Harold, Tommy and Jacko, who had all by this time consumed at least two large glasses of "plonk" and were stepping repeatedly and obliviously on the toes of their reluctant looking partners.

Ladies and gents," announced the M.O, "please put your glasses down and your hands together for the one and only Corporal Bumbling Bill Bailey!"

As the dancers returned to their seats to watch the comic turn, Albert dashed to sit next to Camelina, only to be barged by the sturdy figure of Jabez Hulse.

"Move over Tomlinson," snarled Hulse under his breath.

"You move over," retorted Albert standing his ground, "I was here first."

"Yeah well we all know you've a girl back in Blighty, so you don't need another. Camelina wants me to sit next to her."

"Oh yeah, and have you asked her?"

"I've a better idea," hissed Jabez, "we'll settle it outside."

Stifling a laugh Harold nudged Tommy, "These two are like a couple of children in the playground, I think we'd better keep an eye on them,"

Camelina had said nothing during the muttered but heated exchange that had taken place next to her. Now, as Harold and Tommy slipped out in pursuit of the quarrelling pair, Bill saw someone else sat down next to her. It was Jock. Camelina smiled and turned her sultry eyes towards him obviously enjoying his company.

Bill smiled, what were Albert and Jabez thinking of, fighting for this girl's attention when she had given it to someone else.

Bumbling Bill Bailey having finished his routine, the band had struck up again. Bill saw Jock get his feet, bow courteously and held his hand out to Camelina.

As they moved in time to the music he pressed his cheek close to hers, feeling the warmth and softness of her skin. At the end of the dance they went quickly and without speaking outside.

A few minutes later Bill also came out of the canteen, and looked around for his friends. Half hidden by a tall tree, he saw a couple locked in a passionate embrace, then realised that it was Jock and Camelina.

The next second he heard an accusing voice, "There you are!" and saw Jabez Hulse emerge from the shadows and stride towards the couple. As he came closer he swayed a little, "I'm going to knock your bloody head off!"

Jock looked up and said calmly, "I think you've done enough fighting for one night pal, get to your bed man," and taking Camelina by the arm he began to walk away. As he did so Hulse struck him a glancing blow with his fist, sending Jock sprawling on the ground. Hulse then swung his boot mercilessly, kicking his victim again and again.

"Stop, stop, for God's sake stop," shouted Bill, and ran at him. A second later Jabez Hulse was also lying prone, felled by a punch. Surprised and now perturbed by his own actions, Bill knelt down by both men.

"Jock, Jabez, what the hell – speak to me both of you – oh in Christ's name, speak to me lads!" He stood up and looked around for Camelina, but she was nowhere to be seen.

From the canteen Sergeant Prosser staggered upon the group.

"What's all this then?" he said, leaning unsteadily over the two unconscious young men.

"Thank God it's you Sarge," gasped Bill.

"Are you a party to this Gibson?" slurred Prosser.

"I didn't mean to hurt him -"

"You'll be on a charge."

"You don't understand, I was just trying to -"

"I don't want to hear excuses."

Jabez let out a groan. "Who hit me?" he sat up and rubbed his jaw. Jock was also stirring now.

"Get up Jabey," urged Bill grabbing his arm, "Sarge is here." Jabez glared down at Jock. "It was him wasn't it - I'll do for him once and for all," and shrugging off Bill's arm he raised a fist.

"No you don't lad," intervened Prosser, pushing him away. "Gibson, help this other man up."

As Bill stooped to Jock's side, Jock's comrades, the last to leave, were now rolling out of the canteen, rowdy and very drunk. Seeing their friend being manhandled by a "Sassenach", they immediately came lurching over.

"Who did this to my mate?" demanded Joey, "Was it you sonny?" he seized Bill by the lapels.

"Leave him Joey!" Jock snapped, "He stepped in to help me." He then looked meaningfully at Jabez.

"All right, we don't want any more trouble lads," ordered Prosser, his voice steadier now. "Or you'll all end up on a charge. Go back to your tents and get some rest, you'll need all your spirit for tomorrow." He took Jabez firmly by the arm.

"Sorry pal," Joey said and let go of Bill.

Jock, giving Jabez a parting glare, stumbled slowly away with his comrades. Jabez and Bill were about to do the same, but Sergeant Prosser held them back.

"Any more of this fighting, and you'll both be for the high jump, understand? Kings Regulations are very clear on drunkenness and brawling, and I wouldn't like to see either of you lads go to the bad." Then, smiling he added, "But whoever gave you that fat lip Hulse, should be in the regimental boxing team." He winked at Bill. "Now get some shut eye, you've an early start in the morning."

Just after sunrise, with kitbags, rifles and equipment strapped upon their backs, the soldiers lined up in their units. Bill, Harold and Tommy were next to each other, with Jabez, Albert and Jacko immediately behind.

"Thank goodness it's a nice day," Jacko said adjusting his kitbag once more. "Don't fancy carrying this lot if it's pouring down."

"It won't last," Bill, observed, "Them clouds are too low, it'll be raining in a few hours."

"Well let's hope we get to where we're going before it does." Harold scowled.

"You alright Jabey?" Albert whispered, "You don't half look rough."

"I feel it, and I think my jaw's been dislocated," he said, loud enough for Bill to hear. "Whoever did it could lose 28 days pay under Kings Regulations, for drunkenness alone."

Bill, without turning, retorted, "That'll be the same for you in that case then Jabey."

"Look lads, them blokes have got skirts on." Said Albert.

"I know," sneered Jabez, "That Jock looks a right fool don't he? They all do." He glowered as the Scottish soldiers, in regimental regalia, fell in alongside them. "And if I catch him with my Camelina again, I swear I'll swing for him."

"Oh, stop going on about that," said Jacko, "maybe she doesn't even know how much you like her. Might stop her putting it about."

All the soldiers laughed.

"When I want advice from a kid, I'll ask for it, all right." spat Jabez.

"No talking in the ranks," shouted Prosser, "save your energy for the march. It's a long way to the front. Officer approaching!" The men stood to attention.

Captain Stubbs's voice was calm, measured; "Now men, we'll be marching at a steady pace, two miles per hour. There will be no talking or smoking. We've a job to do at the end, you'll find out more when we get there. In the meantime, any questions?"

Tommy said, "How are we going to know if we're going the right speed sir, the two miles an hour like you said?"

The Captain smiled, "Just try to keep up with whoever's in front of you Fisher – while not treading on their heels." There was laughter in the ranks. "I understand some of you are the worse for wear after last night's ah  entertainments," he smiled again, "but you only have yourselves to blame for that."

"You're right Sir." Said Sergeant Prosser, "And the fresh air and gentle exercise, before we get down to business, will do wonders for them, will it not lads."

"Yes Sarge." They all shouted in unison, "It will, Sarge,"

Stubbs nodded, "On arrival at the trench, we will have further orders, then make it ready for our occupation. If repairs are required, we will undertake to make them. A word of warning, be always vigilant and on the lookout for snipers, and when in your trench on no account raise your head above the parapet unless ordered. The Germans will have their rifles trained along the line, and you will be an easy target. Be alert. Oh and one final thing, remember we will be with other battalions, and we all need to get along and trust one another - we're all on the same side after all."

"Speak for yourself," hissed Jabez under his breath, "I wouldn't trust a Scottie farther than I could throw him."

"Leave it out Jabey," murmured Bill, "they've already seen some fighting, some of us haven't, they can help us."

"I've done my share," retorted Jabez, "I was at Mons don't forget, we were lucky to get out alive. You'll soon see what its all about."

"They say this next skirmish is going to be a piece of cake though," said Harold, "grab the German lines, mop up the village, done and dusted in a couple of days - easy."

Albert grinned, "Let's hope so Harold – then a bit of leave eh?"

"Hey, Jabez, look who's over there," said Tommy.
To their left the nurses had lined up to see the boys off, and at the forefront was Camelina. Jabez gave her a nod, but she turned away, her attention seemingly on another young soldier. Jabez looked to see if Jock had seen her, and as their eyes met, there passed between the two rivals a glimmer of understanding, and what could almost have been the hint of a smile.

"Attention!" yelled Prosser. The click of several hundred boots rang out across the field. "Slooow march!"

"Where is it we're going again Sarge?" Jacko asked

"Neuve Chappell, Wilks, now shut up and march."

## Sunday 11<sup>th</sup> November 1973

"And that was our introduction to the war - Neuve Chapelle." Bill leaned back in the armchair and re-lit his pipe. Taking a deep draw he breathed out again and gazed into the cloud of white smoke as it spread around him. "You see Beattie it was the first time we'd been near a proper trench. We'd heard what those lads had said, seen them wounded soldiers, even heard the guns in the distance, but none of it had seemed real though."

Beattie nodded, "You were still thinking it was all going to be over soon and that you'd be coming home as heroes."

"Not heroes, never that, but coming home, yes, all of us. We knew we might get wounded, but that was all."

"There's wounds and there's wounds I suppose," said Beattie quietly, "and not all of them heal." Bill's eyes widened.

"You never spoke a truer word," he said almost in a whisper. "We never thought of death, not then, but as we got nearer to the front line we saw them - " Bill broke off, his face tense with emotion.

There was silence for a few seconds before Beattie said, "Saw what?"

Bill's voice trembled, "Bodies, laid by the side of the road, not even covered over, then we saw the burial party. Those bodies, they were blokes like us, being dumped in a hole in the ground, in some field, in a foreign bloody country. We soon realised it was going to be no bloody holiday." Bill lowered his head and Beattie saw his knuckles whiten as his clenched fist closed around his pipe.

Beattie reached out and touched his arm. "You don't have to tell me Bill if it makes you…"

He patted her hand. "I do Beattie, I do, they want me to, I want to." Bill was staring into the fire now. "We'd no idea what we'd let ourselves in for, no damned idea at all. Seeing those bodies, laid out like meat on a butcher's slab, that was the moment when we all thought - what the hell had we done that day in the village hall? That recruiting day; if we could have turned the clock back, I'll warrant it would have been a very scene in that hall."

"Yes, yes I'm sure, if you had known the reality of what was waiting for you, none of you would have been so keen."

"Keener to tell the recruiting sergeant where to stick his ruddy papers! They used to say the conchies were just cowards. Now I reckon they were only ones with their heads screwed on. But some of them conchies volunteered to join up, but not to fight, they were sent as stretcher-bearers, going out into no-mans land to get the wounded, some of the bravest lads I've ever seen." Bill sighed heavily. "There we were, soldiers of the King whether we liked it or not, on our way to the front and there was no going back. Somehow we had to make the best of it."

"I'll make us some tea," said Beattie, getting up and filing the kettle. She set out the teacups and poured some milk in each. "Go on if you want Bill."

Bill ignored the rattling teacups and continued. "By the time we reached the trenches the rain had set in. Everywhere you stepped it was filthy slimy mud, you could hardly keep your footing on the duckboards. We were chilled to the marrow, and not surprising because we were soaking wet. Then the guns started, the explosions shaking the ground, on and on, this constant terrifying noise."

"It must have been awful," said Beattie, She poured out the tea and put the cups on the table.

He emptied his pipe into the fire, and placed it on the mantle shelf. "I killed my first German there, stuck my bayonet in him, through his heart, just like we'd done in training, except this wasn't a bag of straw. He didn't make a sound, just dropped on the ground like a rag doll. I stared at this crumpled shape, his eyes staring out, and I couldn't believe what I'd done. It reminded me of when I used to kill rabbits for the pot back home, and how even that made me feel sick. But this – ah." Bill's eyes were moist, staring deeper into the fire. "It was only when Jabez shoved me out of the way and shot the German who was about to shoot me that I came too, and reality sunk in. It was survival, him or me."

Beattie saw the agony in Bill's eyes. She said, "If you hadn't done what you did, if Jabez hadn't - it would have been your mother getting the telegram."

"Why did it have to be either of us though Beattie," said Bill intensely, "why?"

"It would take a wiser woman than me to answer that," said Beattie.

He smiled weakly at her then stared back into the flames." That lot only lasted three days, but in that time we'd gone from young carefree lads that had left England a few months before, to hard-bitten old lags. What we saw and did, we didn't want to repeat but that was inevitable, the war was still raging and as long as we were alive, we were still part of it."

A tear fell from Beattie's eye as she too gazed into the fire, and in the bright flames she saw, as Bill did, the spirits of the young men, Bill's friends and comrades, and the young German and millions like them, the lost generation that had given their lives in the hope of a better world.

"But you got through it," said Beattie

He smiled, "Yes we did, by some bloody miracle, considering the slaughter that took place there and the other places we went to. But what we'd gone through wasn't half as bad as what was yet to come."

# CHAPTER SEVEN

The Somme
30th June. 1916

As evening approached the unbroken line of rhythmically swaying khaki stretched almost as far as the eye could see; battalion upon battalion in close formation, snaking down the country lanes towards the front line. The sky was heavy with rain, which dripped in constant rivulets from the men's newly issued steel helmets.

Somewhere in the middle were Bill, Albert, Tommy, Harold, Jacko and Jabez. The six were 'old sweats' now, and in the last months their young eyes had seen much, too much - of destruction and agony, of mutilated bodies and blood, of men dying of disease and bullet holes, gas and mortar bombs. They had seen fear and courage, anger and despair, and not a little madness, and all these they had felt in themselves, not least fear.

Somehow, by a series of miracles, flukes or occasionally skill and forethought, they were all six still walking upright. Now barely an hour went by without one or other of them, with a mixture of disbelief, thankfulness to the Almighty, and terror of living on borrowed time, remarking on the astonishing fact of his continued existence. Indeed it was a fact that had only grown more astonishing each time the battalion had suffered further heavy fatalities, and new recruits came to take their place, fresh from training and full of all the bluster, bravado and insouciance the six had themselves displayed on first arriving in France.

Last night they had all gone into a nearby town, where, after spending several days pay in a series of cafes, had found themselves – how it had happened none of them could quite remember - in the local brothel, where a businesslike Madame had quickly relieved them of even more money for a 'good time with the girls'. Come the cold light of morning, now marching the rain swept lanes, the only desire left in any of them, was to curl up somewhere soft and warm and go to sleep.

"You all right Jacko?" asked Tommy.

Jacko shook his head, "No mate; got a real bad head."

"Glad to know I'm not the only one then," laughed Tommy. "Should take a leaf out of his book," he nodded towards Captain Stubbs. Straight as a die, and leading from the front, like always. "Don't ask us to do anything he wouldn't, he's a good man."

"In his way I suppose," murmured Jacko

"What do you mean?"

"Some say he's not a proper officer, not a proper gentleman if you know what I mean."

"That's just talk Jacko, don't listen to them rumours, Stubbs is as good as any of them, I trust him. Let's face it, he's never let us down has he."

"Nor has Bill, nor you, nor any of us." Jacko pointed out. Tommy shrugged. "I agree Bill's a good man – as a matter of fact I was bashing his ear in the cafe last night, pouring me heart out about Maggie, and he said I should go ahead and marry her when we get through this."

"If we get through it."

"Now let's not have any of that talk," chipped in Harold.

"Why not?" retorted Jacko, "you were saying the same thing yourself yesterday."

"Ah but that was before I met that lovely lady in town last night. Give me a whole new zest for life she did."

"Not all she give you I don't suppose!" said Jacko.
This set the others roaring with laughter, all except Harold who looked suddenly perturbed.

"Just don't start scratching Harold," said Jacko, "you'll set us all off."
Tommy, who like Jabez, was feeling a twinge of guilt about the night's adventures said, "Oh by the way lads, when we get back to Blighty, you won't say anything to Maggie about where we went will you?"

There was more laughter, then Jacko said, "Don't worry Tom, we all want an invitation to the wedding, though don't make me do the best man speech – a few ales and I'll be telling the whole story, with a few embellishments. But like I say, that's if we make it." Jacko's expression darkened again. "They say that somewhere out there, everyone's got a bullet with their name on, it's just a matter of time."

Seeing Tommy looking saddened by this, Bill said, "Don't listen to him mate, he's just a right morbid sod sometimes. We'll be all right, and so will you and Maggie."

Albert, reminded of his own part in the adventure, grinned from ear to ear, "Mimi was lovely," he said wistfully. "Best night of my life." He remembered how Mimi had cuddled up to him and, how, after his third glass of brandy he had confessed his fear of dying, she had told him how brave and handsome he was. Such simple words, on her sweet, beautiful lips, had transformed him; never before had he felt so proud, so manly.

"She said I looked like a prince in a fairy tale."

Harold and Bill stifled a laugh.

"What about Emma?" Bill asked.

Albert looked serious, "She's in Blighty."

"Exactly."

"Exactly," repeated Albert, as if this proved some logical point.

"You sure Mimi said that?" asked Harold, "about you being like a prince?"

"You don't forget something like that," said Albert, still starry eyed. "I'll always remember Mimi."

"And she'll always remember you too, of course," said Harold, winking at Bill. "She's probably thinking of you right now, holding her hand to her cheek that you kissed so fondly, calling out your name every night in her sleep – Albert, Albert, come back to me some day darling – and bring me more of that lovely money of yours -"

Albert frowned, "Here, you're taking the Mickey out of me."

"Me? Never."

"Yeah, pack it in Harold," said Bill, "a man can dream can't he?"

"Albert certainly can."

"Anyway Harold," chipped in Jacko, "you're a fine one to talk."

"Meaning what?"

"I think he's talking about that girl that dragged you up the stairs."

"She did no such thing," said Harold indignantly.

"No?"

"No, I went of my own accord."

---

They all laughed.

"Unlike some, I can hold my liquor," went on Harold. "I remember every minute of last night."

"You'll remember Fred Carter then," smiled Bill.

"Who?"

"A rookie we were drinking with. He helped us catch you when you fell down the stairs, and good job too, you'd be on a stretcher this morning if not."

"I thought it was Tommy," said Harold vaguely.

"He was as in as bad a state as you."

"I wasn't," protested Tommy. "Just drowning me sorrows that's all – I do miss Maggie."

"Don't be such a wet lettuce," said Jabez contemptuously "Albert's got the right idea. Carpe Diem."

"What?" said Albert.

"It means, "seize the day". We're stuck out here in this muddy hell hole, not knowing when or if that bullet with our name on is coming our way – the least we deserve is to enjoy ourselves while we can. And if in the end the good Lord decides to spare us and send us back to Blighty, no one's going to blame us for forgetting our fears in a few hours snatched pleasure."

"Emma would," said Albert anxiously.

"To hell with Emma," said Jabez, "to hell with all women, they're only good for one thing."

"How dare you say that about my Emma!" said Albert angrily.

"Why? Its only what you were saying about her last night."

"I was not!"

"In a manner of speaking you were – as soon as that French tart started whispering sweet nothing in your ear -"

"How dare you say that about Mimi!"

"And then when she dropped her drawers -"

"Oi! You lot, that's enough of that!" barked Sergeant Prosser. "I will not have profanity in the ranks."

The men fell silent for a second then Jabez ventured, "How did you get on last night by the way Sarge?

"How do you mean?" said Prosser guardedly.

"Thought I saw you slipping up the stairs of a certain establishment with a young lady companion -"

Prosser coughed noisily, "I did take the opportunity to acquaint myself with some of the locals if that's what you mean, in the interests of goodwill – they are our allies after all."

"Here Sarge," said Harold, "are you itching or something? You keep scratching yourself."

"No, no, just these new uniforms; take a bit of wearing in, irritates the skin."

"Oh," said Harold archly, "glad its not just me. For a minute I thought you might have picked up something nasty in town last night."

Prosser coughed again, said sternly, "Right let's have no more talking in the ranks," and marched on ahead.

"Poor old Sarge," laughed Harold. "Still, its put a spring in his step this morning. "You should have picked a girl out last night Bill, would have done you the world."

"He's saving himself," said Jacko.

"Who for?"

"That'd be telling," said Bill.

The truth was he had been tempted to join his friends, to get drunk and spend his pay on an hour or two of female company. The girls they had met in town, despite being "tarts" as the men called them, had all been very pretty, and his body had ached with all the impulses natural to a young man. But there was also a streak of the puritan in Bill, and he felt strongly that love in every sense of the word was a precious thing, and should not be squandered, bought or sold.

The cafe had been full of soldiers, new recruits and old sweats like themselves. Content with just one small glass of beer, he had sat at a table by the window with Tommy and watched the evenings antics play out before him. After a rousing sing song led by Sergeant Prosser, Jabez, Jacko and a good few others, most of the men had drunk themselves silly. He had smiled as Albert and a more terrified Harold had ascended the stairs with the two French girls, and even more at Sergeant Prosser's attempts to do so secretly. What would Emma think of Albert if she knew? And what if, as his father maintained, it was he whom Emma truly cared for? Much as Bill tried to resist this thought, he found it undeniably seductive.

He had then listened to Tommy's drunken ramblings on the love of his life, his darling Maggie. Bill hoped sincerely that Tommy would marry the young woman, for he could tell it was the kind of love that should not be wasted. But then who could say what would be? The fate of all of them was in God's hands. Then in the midst of all the commotion he had noticed a young boy sitting alone at the end of the table. He had seemed a quiet young fellow, overwhelmed by the noise and bawdiness. Bill had motioned to him to come over. "Sit here lad," he had said indicating a chair, "what's your name?"

"Fred Carter, I've just joined a few months ago."

"Must be with our lot then Fred, we've got some new recruits. I'm Bill, this here's Tommy."
Tommy had lifted his rheumy eyes briefly from gazing at his photograph of Maggie, nodded to Fred, and taking another swig of beer, resumed his reverie.

"And that pile of uniforms in the corner, is our sergeant James Prosser, Private Jabez Hulse and Private Jacko Wilkes."

"Looks like they're having a good time," Fred had smiled.

"In a way, but I doubt they'll remember much in the morning."

"I've heard some of the things you lads have been through," Fred had said. "I suppose it must affect you."

"Let's just say, it makes you value life in a new kind of way."

It was at this point that Harold had emerged from the room above and teetered on the top step of the stairs. Seeing him about to lose his balance Bill and Fred had raced quickly up, catching him just in time.

After sitting Harold safely down in a corner of the cafe, the two rescuers shook hands. "Thanks for your company," Fred had said, "I enjoyed out chat, I hope to see you again."

"Next town we get to, we'll have a beer together, but a quiet one!"

"I'd like that Bill."

"Good luck to you mate."

Night had fallen. The pounding of the big guns, still invisible but grown steadily louder over the last few miles, was now uncomfortably close.

Captain Stubbs stood at the side of the road and watched his men as they passed. They were visibly weary, rain sodden, and apprehensive. Ahead of them now were the trenches.

"Single file along the trench till we find our section," called out Stubbs, "then make ready for inspection."

A chorus of complaint ran along the line. "We're knackered," protested Albert, "when do we get some sleep?"

"When I say so," Sergeant Prosser snapped, "and not before." Then turning to Captain Stubbs he said, "Tomlinson's right if you'll permit me sir, the men are dog tired."

"I know that Sergeant, it's been a long march. When we get to our section let them take shifts getting their heads down. Though if they can sleep through this noise, they must be well and truly spent."

Sporadic machine gun fire had now started up alongside the regular pom-pom of the artillery. At that moment there was a loud crack and a sudden bright light as a shell burst directly overhead, sending the men diving for cover.

"That was a close call," said Stubbs. "Better get our chaps in right away."

The rain was still falling, the ground around the line softened and slippery. Captain Stubbs and Sergeant Prosser walked the long section of the trench, directing the deployment of planks and tarpaulins as makeshift shelters. When every man was in, they settled themselves into the officers" dugout.

"Remarkably dry in here considering," observed Stubbs, He lit an oil lamp, took off his cap and cape and sat on the wooden chair by the desk.

"Give me your jacket Sir," said Prosser, "it needs drying out."

"Thank you Sergeant." The Captain looked around the earth stained planks illuminated by the lamp, "Well, here we are again eh, another home from home, if that's not exaggerating a little." Taking out a silver case he offered Prosser a cigarette.

Smoke curled around the small space as the two men sat in silence. After a moment Stubbs looked at his pocket watch,

—

"Midnight," he said, "7 hours till first light."
"Will the order to attack be issued then sir?"
"I am expecting as much."
"And then?"
"Who knows Sergeant, who knows?"
"Very true sir."
"We've been lucky so far."
"Yes, though perhaps its not luck but -"
"Sergeant do you believe in God?"
Sergeant Prosser nodded, "Do you think he's on our side Sir?
A misty look came into the Captain's eyes, "I would…like to believe so." Then more briskly he said, "Look you get some rest, I'll keep watch, I'll take Gibson, Fisher and Braithwaite on a night patrol, we've got to make sure the wire's in place."
"But Sir you need the rest, for the morning, I'll take the men."
"Perhaps you're right. Very good…. thank you Sergeant."

When Prosser had left, Captain Stubbs began to unpack his kit, laying out each item in a regular fashion, as he had been taught. He caught sight of his face in the small mirror hung from one of the overhead supports. He looked gaunt, tired, and was in need of a shave. This would 'never do' for a real gentleman, he reflected wryly. How dare they tell us how to behave, he thought with a sudden bitterness. A 'temporary gentleman' was what the traditional officer class called the likes of him, or more flatteringly one of 'the chosen ones', but beneath it was usually contempt, sometimes even open derision. Thank God he had not been alone to face those scathing remarks, and the taunts.
He had not wanted any of this. Coming from a working class background he knew he had to enlist and would have joined the ranks, but he had been sought after. With such a shortage, educated men had been sorely needed to lead the troops, and as a teacher he had indeed been deemed officer material – but he had little illusions about how the *'real'* officers regarded him, and the equal level of resentment that often came from his own class within the ranks, who thought he had got above his station. "Temporary or not" he said to his reflection "We still stand together in this God forsaken war."

As for the ageing generals and dunderheads who had presumed to instruct him in the arts of warfare, what did they know about what really went on out here – the men gassed and blinded, blown apart and falling at your side, the screams of agony. It was the stuff of nightmare, and for what, a few miserable miles of ground?

From the pages of his bible he drew out a photograph. His darling wife Olivia, and his two young children, Maisie and George gazed serenely out at him. If he could have one wish, one answered prayer in the whole of his life, it would be to be with them now. Tears now filling his eyes, he sat at the desk, took pen and paper and began to write.

*My Dearest Olivia,*

*I hope this letter finds you and the children well. I think of you at all times, and look forward with all my heart to the day we shall be reunited. I pray that it may be soon. Out here the men are of stout heart, and despite the difficulties we find ourselves in, keep faith, as I do, that God will see fit to deliver us home safely to our families. You fill my waking thoughts my darling, and I desire so desperately for you to likewise fill my arms.*

*You will have heard no doubt of the dangers and the fate that has befallen many of our chaps; when you read of such things my dearest, I beg you not to be alarmed or be prey to despair or fear for me; I am blessed with a hardy and most competent company of men, and we look after one another in every respect, of that you can be assured. Therefore please think of me not with anxiety, but only with happiness in your heart. Our love will not allow us to part, of that I am certain.*

*Tell Maisie to practice every day on the piano, for I shall want to hear her beautiful playing when I return. Also warn George that if he breaks any more windows with his football I expect him to repair them himself; I shall buy him a fishing rod when I get back, and we will bring back a veritable shoal of trout from the stream for tea! And so my darling I must close now; be of good cheer my dearest one...*

At that moment Sergeant Prosser reappeared and stepped inside the hut. "We're going out now Sir," he said "Should be about half an hour all being well, once we've got out bearings."

"You've got the wire cutters?"

Sergeant Prosser nodded, "they're in here Sir," he patted the equipment pouch strapped to his belt.

"Very Good Sergeant, go far as you can. The artillery should do the rest.

"Yes Sir that will give us a clear run, tomorrow." He looked at his watch. "Sir, its now 0.30 hours, you agree?"

Stubbs quickly folded the unfinished letter, slipped it into his bible with the photograph and looked at his watch; he nodded in agreement.

"Sergeant," said Captain Stubbs quietly as the sergeant turned to leave.

"Yes Sir?"

"Bring them all back."

Sergeant Prosser smiled, "I will Sir, I will."

# CHAPTER EIGHT

1st July 1916

There had been a murmuring, unsettled atmosphere in the trench all night. Despite their fatigue, the men had found it hard to rest. The tin oil lamps and candles, wedged at intervals into the mud walls cast flickering shadows in the amber light. Bill and his friends had also lit a small fire in the brazier, drawing comfort from the crackle and glow. Yet even the sentry on the fire step seemed more nervous than usual.

After a short but nerve-wracking night patrol, Bill had managed to snatch a couple of precious hours sleep, in one of the dug out niche's in the trench wall, but though still tired, there was no chance of any more, he was too keyed up, every sinew alert, waiting. He looked at his watch: 2am. A few more hours – and what then? He gazed up at the sky. It was a clear night, the rain clouds gone to reveal a thousand stars in the blanket of inky blue. Would he see them again tomorrow night? And what about the next? Some said that a man's fate was written in the stars.

"Come on lads, get those letters done." Sergeant Prosser appeared followed by a young soldier. "This is Private Carter," said Prosser, "One of our new recruits, he's with us now, so look after him."

"Hello mate," said Bill, "we meet again."

"Oh, Bill, yeah, I remember," Fred shook his hand, "no chance of that quiet beer we promised ourselves just yet then, eh."

"It'll keep for us Fred, it'll keep, just as soon as this lot's over."

"Will we keep for it though," came a voice from the shadows.

"Take no notice of Jacko," said Bill, "one of our resident optimists. Budge up Jacko and let Fred take the weight off."
Jacko moved along the plank and Fred sat next to him.
Suddenly the trench was rocked by a deafening bang shaking the timbers and setting the tin mugs rattling. Seconds after the men had dived instinctively for cover, a shower of muddy earth rained down on them. After half a minute they got slowly to their feet again.

"You all right mate," said Bill, offering Fred a steadying hand.

"Blimey," said Fred, "how close was that?"

"Not that close at all," Harold assured him, brushing mud from his battledress, "the Bosch are like thunder, always sound like they're coming down on top of you, but they're really miles away." Jacko laughed cynically.

"Well, maybe not miles," admitted Harold.

"When I was a nipper I always used to hide under the bed when it thundered." said Fred.

"That's what we need now I reckon," said Harold, "a great big feather bed we can all get under."

"A bomb proof bed," said Tommy.

"With half a dozen French girls in it!" said Albert.

A wave of ribald laughter ran along the trench. When it had died down, the low, repetitive thud of artillery could be heard.

"Not more shells?" said Fred.

"Yeah, but this time they're ours son," said Sergeant Prosser, "it's the big guns retaliating, battering the Bosch before we go over."

"What's it like Sarge - going over the top?" Fred asked. The Sergeant drew a breath before replying. "Keep your head low and keep moving, don't stop for anyone. And when you meet the Germans you shoot "em, stab "em with that bayonet." He assumed the pose and lunged with an imaginary gun. "Just like your training."

"Except it won't be a sack of straw," said Jacko grimly.

"I'd like to stab these bloody rats," Tommy grimaced, "but they're too bloody quick, I hate them bloody things, if they're not eating your food, they're having a go at you." He stamped his foot irritably as something moved over his boot.

"I know what to do," said Fred, "but how does it *feel* going out there."

"Best not to think about it," advised Albert. "Too much thinking is not good, not for the likes of us. Leave the thinking to the generals."
Jacko snorted, "And you think they know what they're doing? You think they care about us?"

"I would bleeding hope so!" said Albert.
Jacko shook his head in silent disdain.

There was quiet for a moment, each man lost in his own thoughts. Another thundering explosion rent the air, this time they barely moved. Sergeant Prosser nudged back the cuff of his tunic. "Twenty past two," he said quietly to himself, almost as if awaiting a train at some sleepy country railway station. Then louder, he said, "Right, Who's written their letter?" No one answered. "Then get to it."

The men, uttering a collective sigh, took out notepaper and pencils and bent their heads in thought.

Fred turned to Bill and whispered, "Why does he want us to write letters home now?"

"Um – well," hesitated Bill, "its just a good time I suppose - while we've an hour or two on our hands like -"

As Fred stared at Bill in the dim lamplight, the expression in the new recruit's eyes suddenly changed; of course, he knew why. Bill pursed his lips. "Who will you write to Fred?"

"My mother -" then almost apologetically, "I haven't got a girl see, well, not a regular one -"

"That's all right Fred, it's your letter."

"What shall I write?"

Sergeant Prosser placed a hand on Fred's shoulder, "Have you ever told your mother you love her?"

Fred hung his head. "No. Sarge I haven't."

"Then tell her son, tell her now."

Tommy Fisher said, "Sarge, how do you spell where we are?"

"W - H - E - R - E - W - E - A - R - E...." chanted Harold. The others laughed with a forced jollity.

"All right, very funny," grinned Tommy, leaning over to cuff his mate's ear. "I mean this place, where we are! What's it called, the Somme?"

"Can't put nothing like that in lad," Sergeant Prosser ordered. "Nothing about our position, if that got out -" he gave a low whistle. "Just write about yourself Fisher, as if it were, so to speak, the last -" He left the sentence unfinished.

The young soldiers stared at him, not daring to look at one another. Tommy Fisher broke the silence, "Better not be Sarge," he said with a nervous laugh, "Still got a lot to do."

Jabez turned to Fred, "You a volunteer mate?"

"Yeah, joined up a few months ago. Could have gone in the navy but I wanted to join the army like my dad. Mother didn't want me to go but I felt I had to, to follow Dad. She's on her own now with our Walter, my kid brother, he's only six."

"Where is your dad, son?" asked Sergeant Prosser

"He went to Gall i poli last year, got through all right, but not heard much from him since."

"It's Gallipoli mate, Gallipoli – not Gall I poli." laughed Albert.

Fred looked embarrassed. Sergeant Prosser put his hand on the boy's shoulder again, and with an effort to hold back his emotions said quietly, "That's where my boys went. My Doris wanted me to go with them, but I told her, it's not up to me. I wish I could have though – I might have been able to save them." He turned away and sat down.

The men exchanged more silent glances. No one spoke. Jabez took out a small brass tin of rolled cigarettes. "Smoke Sarge?" Prosser nodded gratefully. "You Fred?"

"Thanks."

Jabez took a lighter from his tunic pocket and offered it to Fred. Jacko began to laugh, "That's his lucky lighter; one of the Mademoiselles from the town gave it to him."

"She gave him more than that or so I hear." Tommy Fisher smirked at Jabez, who gave him a hostile look, but resisted rising to the bait.

"No chance of you getting anything Tom," said Harold. Tommy took a slightly crumpled photograph from his pocket and waved it. "You're right, I've got my girl; I don't need your Frenchie women."

Harold suddenly grabbed the photo from Tommy's hand. "I see what you mean, isn't she lovely lads," he jested, and passed it to Sergeant Prosser.

"Here, give it back," shouted Tommy indignantly, lunging to retrieve the photo.

"Bit too good for him I reckon," said Jacko, holding Tommy back, "What do you think Sarge?"

Prosser nodded, "She's certainly a pretty girl - where did you find her Fisher?"

"Give it me back Sarge, please," pleaded Tommy, "that's all I got of her."

Prosser, looking slightly ashamed now handed it back.

"Soldiers coming through!" came a shout, as a line of men, laden with kit and rifles began filing through. The lads pressed themselves against the mud walls to let them pass,

"There's a lot of us here" Jacko said, "More than I've seen before."

Harold nodded "It's the big push, that's what they're calling it."

"Bloody hell, if it not it's Ernie Fowles!" Jacko exclaimed. Hearing his name, the young man stepped from the line and shook Jacko's hand enthusiastically. "Hey up mate, fancy seeing you lot here."

Albert patted Ernie on the back, "Last time I saw you mate, you was skulking out of the village hall the day we all joined up." Ernie turned hesitantly towards Albert, "Ah, well, yeah -"

"He must have run out of newspapers," said Harold, "or excuses more like." They all laughed.

"Fowles, get back in line," shouted his sergeant who happened to be bringing up rear and checking for stragglers. Ernie hurried back to the line, "No, just luck," he uttered, "I'll come back and tell you all about it."

The men settled back down on the benches again. Albert lit a cigarette

"That should be some story." He pondered, "Can't wait to hear it."

"He's a right lad," Jacko laughed, "His cheek will get him through, mark my words."

"But how come he's here, if anyone could have got out of this lot he should have been able to." Harold said.

Bill sat on the bench, staring down at the muddy earth. Harold nudged his elbow, "Penny for 'em mate."

"Oh, I was thinking about home,"

"Yeah me too,"

"I was thinking about when I was a kid, Dad worked at Henshaw's farm. He was a herdsman there."

"Yes I know, he used to get me ma eggs every Sunday. They were really good, them yolks were really yellow, Oh Bill you're making me hungry now."

Bill smiled. "Me too, could just eat one of them boiled with a nice slice of bread toasted on the fire."

"Stop it Bill, we've only got this bully beef and them damn hard biscuits that could break your teeth on to look forward to." They both laughed and Harold nudged him again. "Carry on then mate, what else were you thinking about."

"In the summer after school, when the nights were light, they'd be gathering in the hay and Dad would let me and our Elsie ride on the cart. Sometimes he'd let me ride on the horse. That's when I realised what strong, beautiful and gentle animals they are. I often think about Dolly and Bess, wonder where they are. I hope they're looked after and treated better than some of the poor creatures I've seen here."

"Hey up lads, how are you all?" Ernie, hands in his trouser pockets and a cigarette hanging from the corner of his mouth, sauntered along the trench towards them put down his kit bag and sat down next to Tommy.

"So where've you been Ern?" Bill asked.
Ernie sighed and stubbed out his cigarette in the mud. "Mopping up." He said quietly, "Burying them poor sods, we dug graves, long deep holes, then we buried them,Welsh, English, Scots, Irish, even Germans, altogether."
Tommy frowned, "You mean, all of 'em together, in one grave, that's not right, not very respectful."

"There were so many, too many to count. Most of 'em were unrecognisable, the rats had got to them not much left of 'em after them rats had finished.  It was horrible. And the smell..." Ernie shook his head trying to dispel the terrible, harrowing vision which by now was firmly embedded in his thoughts.
The stunned silence reflected in every face. They could  barely lift their heads, engulfed in their own visions of what they had just heard.

It was Ernie who broke the deafening silence. "Before putting them in the ground we emptied their pockets, tied the pay books and tags to the bayonets and stuck 'um in the ground as a marker... Then left them there.

The padre followed behind saying prayers and blessing the graves.  What a bloody mess..."
Again no one spoke.

"But I'm still here." Said Ernie lightening the mood, "And so are you lot, that's a blessing in itself."

"So, what happened exactly, why are you here, I thought you'd have done anything to get out of this." asked Albert'

Ernie leaned in, and lowering his voice said, "Strictly between our selves, it was this conscription lark."

"How do you mean?" said Harold.

"Well I thought - if I got married, they might not call me up."

"So you didn't get married then?

"No, I did get married!"

Tommy was not quite puzzled. "So how come you're here then -"

"It's a long story."

Jacko laughed, "Well we're not going anywhere mate so carry on."

"You see lads, I married Nancy Brittleton."

Harold, Tommy, Albert Jacko and Bill stared open-mouthed.

"Not Nancy from the tripe shop?" said Harold incredulously.

"I thought she was a bit choosy though," snorted Jacko, "only went for men in trousers, aged between 16 and 60!"

There was more loud laughter.

"Well, I thought it was good idea," lamented Ernie, "she was always keen on me, I used to take her me unsold papers to wrap the tripe in. We talked about branching out, starting a fish and chip shop together."

"A match made in heaven," swooned Tommy, rolling his eyes comically.

"I know she's no oil painting, but she didn't seem a bad girl really."

"Really?" the others chorused.

"Not till I married her."

"Let us try to contain our amazement," said Harold.

"It was - do this, - do that, - wipe your feet, nagging me every minute of the day. Couldn't stand it any longer. A fortnight after the wedding I went up the recruiting office and signed up."

"Nearest one's ten miles away," pointed out Tommy

"I biked it."

"So here you are being a soldier." Albert grinned.

"Yeah, here I am. I think its what they call 'the lesser of two evils'."

"Well, welcome Ern," said Harold warmly, "and we promise never to mention tripe again."

Ernie laughed along with the rest of them. Then in a more serious tone he said, "So it looks like I'll be made a man of after all – we all will, one way or another."

The others nodded quietly at these last words. Harold broke the sombre silence, "Meanwhile, I heard a rumour there's a bottle or two of brandy coming our way. That's what we need, warm the cockles of our hearts! Stay and have a tot with us Ern."

"I'd better get back to my lot," demurred Ernie, "don't want to get in trouble."

"You're married to Nancy Brittleton," said Jabez, "there's not much worse can befall you now."

"Oh yes there is." said Ernie sadly, "After this lots over, I've got to go back to her."

At this even Sergeant Prosser laughed.

"All right," said Ernie "You talked me into it." He opened the flap on his kit bag and took out his tin mug.

"C'mon, where's that brandy Sarge?" said Jabez "let's have a drink...."

"Sorry lads, there's only tea for now. Make the most of it, we've not got much left." Sergeant Prosser removed the tin of boiling water from the makeshift stove and poured it into a can, stirred it around and poured the hot weak tea into each man's tin cup.

Bill watched Ernie sipping the tea. There was a change in his friend. That cheeky young lad who had sidled out of the village hall that autumn day now seemed older, even vulnerable. He was still bragging, blustering, still playing the carefree rover, but wherever he had been and whatever he had done had certainly changed him. Then there was the question of Nancy.

Bill's sister Elsie had heard a rumour that they had been seen walking out together but when she had asked him he had denied it. Now he had married her.

Bill moved across the trench and sat next to Ernie. "Shove up mate"

"You alright Bill?" asked Ernie, making room for his friend

"I am mate," Bill grinned.

"So what's up?"

"Nothing, but I know why you married Nancy."

Ernie frowned. "I've told you why, to get out of this lot."

Bill shook his head, "No you didn't mate, you could have had the pick of all the girls, but you chose Nancy? It doesn't make any sense. I think you love her,"

---

"Keep your voice down, they'll hear you. I've got a reputation to live up to you know."

"Oh I know Ern, you were always a charmer."

"That's what Nancy says." Ernie's broad grin said it all.

"I'm right, I knew I was, you *do* love her."

"Well er… I..er…" spluttered Ernie, looking suitably embarrassed. "I suppose I…do…"

"Don't worry mate, she's a good woman, she'll make you happy."

Ernie smiled, "She does," he whispered, "I wish I was with her now." He gripped Bill's hand. "If I don't make it Bill, if I don't get through all this …promise me you'll tell her how much I wanted to come home to her, how much I miss her. Tell her I love her; love her with all my heart. Promise me Bill, promise you'll do that for me."

"Don't think like that mate…"

His grip tightened on Bill's hand. "Promise me Bill, you'll tell her, promise me…." There was urgency in his words.

"I promise Ernie, if I get through this, I'll tell her…"

He broke off as a deafening explosion rent the air above their heads. Ernie released Bill's hand and stood up. "I'd better get back to my unit," he said,

"All right Ern, we'll see you next time" Tommy said

"Last one in Paris is a sissy!" said Jabez

Ernie dusted himself down, picked up his kitbag and shook hands quickly with each of them. "See you again lads, God willing." He gave a spirited, cheeky smile then scurried, half crouched, along the trench, turned the corner and was gone.

Shells were bursting thick and fast now, while corresponding fire from the British lines grew louder. Sergeant Prosser said, "Get those letters finished off lads, and check your rifles, a dirty one won't save your life."

He took Fred's gun and holding it to one of the lamps, inspected the barrel closely, then handed it back to him. "All right we'll see if that brandy's arrived. Bill, do the honours."

Bill Gibson leaned his rifle against the trench wall and walked quickly to the covered dugout at the far end. He knocked on the makeshift wooden door.

"Enter."

In the amber glow, Captain Stubbs was sat at his desk writing. He put down his pen. "Yes Gibson, what is it?"

"Sir, Sergeant Prosser wants to know, if the brandy has arrived."

Captain Stubbs shook his head. "No, not yet. Tell me have you all written your letters home?"

"Yes Sir we have – except Tommy - Private Fisher – he's just finishing his now."

"Well – so am I as a matter of fact. Very well Gibson, I'll come and collect them in a moment, and we'll have to make do with the rum." He smiled kindly, his eyes full of sympathy, of intense, unspoken feelings.

"Thank you Sir," Bill saluted, turned smartly and marched out.

Captain Stubbs gazed after him for a moment. He then read his letter through again, looked longingly at the photograph of his family, and the tears that he had held back for so long, now flowed. Gathering himself, he sealed the letter in an envelope, then took out a handkerchief and cleaned his face. He looked in the mirror and thought, almost with fascination, what strange emotions love and fear were; for he felt both in equal measure now, and felt them strongly – but was the fear for himself, or fear for Olivia and the children, of what they would suffer if… there was fear for his men too, so young, their whole lives ahead of them, but for how long? He must show courage now - whatever was in his heart, courage must be summoned. Speaking to his reflection he said: "Damn this war, and damn the monsters that started it –"

# CHAPTER NINE

A Clear Blue Summers Day

When Bill returned he sensed the mood in the trench had changed. A heavy, uneasy silence had descended. Though they were all seasoned soldiers now, there was something very different about this place, the Somme, something depressing and hopeless, and they could all feel it.

The shelling of the German frontline had continued unabated. With no respite from the constant noise, the men, weary, tired and hungry, sat quietly side by side on the bare planks that lined the trench, each wrapped in his private thoughts. Any high spirits, any hopes of seeing their loved ones, or the green fields of England, were falling away, and in their place a chill fear of what the coming hours might bring gripped their hearts.

"There's no brandy, but he's bringing the rum in a few minutes," Bill said, trying his best to sound cheerful, but hearing his words fall dully against the thud of the guns. "He'll collect the letters too." He joined Albert, Harold, Jabez Jacko, Fred and Sergeant Prosser on the benches.

"Why didn't they send the biscuits?" moaned Albert, who had been polishing his rifle butt for the last half hour. "Not much to ask for, a tin of bloody biscuits."

Harold clicked the barrel of his gun in place. "Tea," he muttered sullenly, "a packet of tea, that's all I want. You took my last ration Bert, but when do I get it back, that's what I'd like to know?"

Albert stopped his cleaning. "When I get some tea sent to me - not my fault it didn't come."

Harold, like a dog with a rabbit, would not let the matter lie, "So I've got to drink this filthy water, because you took my last ration!" The two men stood up suddenly, squared up to one another in angry confrontation.

"Come on now lads," said Bill, putting himself between them, "let's not fall out amongst ourselves, we need to stick together, we need each other, especially now."

Albert and Harold, looking stubborn and unforgiving still, reluctantly sat down and turned their backs on one another in silence. Sergeant Prosser looked at his watch. "An hour to go lads, best get ready."

The men looked from one to the other and gripped their rifles. Suddenly Albert threw his weapon down.

"I'm sick of all this," he said bitterly, "we've been duped, lied to, and that Captain was the one who did it. And now there's no way we can get out of this unholy, bloody, awful mess." He began to cry. Bill, after some hesitation, put his arm around his shoulder. "Come on mate," he said gently, "we all feel the same."

Albert shrugged off Bill's arm, "We're going to die," he said loudly, "all of us, going to die - today, tomorrow, next week, doesn't matter when. If the bloody Hun don't get us, our own bloody lot will. Listen to them," he put his hands over his ears, "that blasted shelling, I can't stand it any more."

Bill guided his friend to the bench and sat next to him. "Calm down Albert, we're all scared, every one of us."

Albert began to sob again. "We're goners Bill, oh God help us."

"Pull yourself together Tomlinson!" said Prosser sharply. "Any more of that talk and you'll be on a charge."

"He'll settle down Sarge." Bill said quietly.

"He'd better."

Albert was shaking uncontrollably now. Harold meanwhile was staring into space, while Fred, picking up on Albert's mood, had also begun to tremble. Jacko and Tommy were stood motionless as the guns roared. No one spoke. Bill lifted his eyes towards the sky; the stars had disappeared now in the coming dawn and the drifting smoke.

Every so often, a particularly loud explosion brought a shower of soil raining down into the trench. Soon it would be time to climb the ladders and go out there, and pray to God they could stay alive – just for one moment, one hour, or one day more.

At 7am Captain Andrew Stubbs made his way along the trench. Daylight had seemed to intensify the noise of the artillery, the ground around them shaking as volley after volley went over, but now the guns had fallen silent.

"Officer approaching!" barked Sergeant Prosser as the young man neared, in his hand the promised bottle of rum. At his approach the men stood to attention.

"At ease," said Stubbs. "Got your tins ready?" The men proffered their drinking vessels. Stubbs's hand trembled noticeably as he poured a modest measure to each. Sergeant Prosser stepped forward, "Let me Sir?"

Stubbs nodded, "Thank you Sergeant." Prosser took the bottle and completed the ritual. Stubbs fidgeted nervously with his pistol in its waist holder as the men imbibed the rum.

"Not joining us Sir?" asked Bill?

Stubbs shook his head.

"What time are we going over Sir?" asked Tommy.

"In half an hour,"

"Is that why them guns has stopped Sir? So as we have a clear run"

"Yes Fisher."

"After all that week long bombardment there shouldn't be any of the Germans left Sir, isn't that what the higher ups say?"

"Anymore lip from you Fisher and I'll put you on a charge." Sergeant Prosser said angrily.

"Yes Sarge. But could you do it before we go over."

"Not a chance of that young man, you'll go with the rest of us."

"Come along men, get your rifles at the ready." Said Captain Stubbs.

The men obediently re-checked their weapons.

"Not like you said back home Sir," ventured Harold boldly, "You and that William Ikin made this lark sound like a piece of cake."

Captain Stubbs stared at Harold, seemingly about to challenge him, then appeared to think better of it. "Have you all finished your letters?" he said quickly.

"Just Fisher to complete his Sir – Fisher, hurry up!" Sergeant Prosser handed over the other letters and Stubbs took them from him. His hands were still shaking. Tommy took from his pocket his unfinished letter, read what he had written so far, then took out a pen and continued.

"Sergeant," said Stubbs, "come along with me a moment." The sergeant followed his superior to the trench HQ. "I've just had confirmation we are in the first wave." Stubbs voice trembled and the two men looked at each other.

"Very good Sir," he said, "Is there anything else?"

"No," answered Captain Stubbs, "Just - good luck out there." Sergeant Prosser saluted, "Thank you Sir, the same to you."

Alone again, Captain Stubbs put his men's letters into a canvas bag. Then from his Bible, he took his letter and the photograph of Olivia. Tears fell from his eyes as he kissed her image. Adding his own letter to the bag he sealed it, then gazing fondly at Olivia's picture one more time returned it between the pages of the Bible and placed the book on his desk. He looked at his watch. It was 7.20 am, ten minutes to go. Dabbing his eyes he removed his pistol, checked it and opened the door.

Captain Stubbs walked the line. The ladders were all in place now, spaced at intervals along the trench. The men stood to attention again as he passed. Seeing him approach, Fred was about to salute, but Stubbs, extending a hand, pressed his arm gently down. "There's no need Fred, not now," he said quietly, surprising the lad by the use of his Christian name. He looked at his watch. "Right men – stand ready!"

As the men stood in an orderly fashion along the sandbagged wall of the trench, Albert slumped back down, his head in his hands. "Get up mate," hissed Jacko, "Before the Sarge sees you." Jacko then stepped over, grabbed Albert by the arms, and dragging him to his feet, thrust his rifle into his hands. Trembling, Albert clung on to the rifle, leaning heavily against the wall.

Bill now turned to Fred, "You alright pal?"

The young man shook his head, shivering uncontrollably. "I can't stop shaking… I'm going to be sick… I can't do this Bill. I can't go, I've got to get away." He recoiled from the wall as if it were on fire. Bill grasped his tunic and pulled him back into line.

"Listen mate we've all got to get through this," he implored his friend, "you've got to go, you stand more chance out there than in here - stay here and one of them will shoot you." He nodded towards Sergeant Prosser and Captain Stubbs, who had both noticed Fred's behaviour. "Just follow me mate, it's just a short walk… that's all, a short walk." He gripped Fred's arm.

"What's that?" said Bill.

"Silence," replied Jacko, "forgotten what it sounds like?"

"No, no," said Bill, "it's a bird – it sounds like a lark."

Captain Stubbs put his head on one side, "You're right Gibson, it is a lark." The men listened, spellbound for a moment to the solitary, beautiful song of the bird.

Stubbs looked at this watch, and nodded to Sergeant Prosser.

"Fix - bayonets!" bawled Prosser.

Albert began to moan and slip down the trench wall again. Jacko pulled him up. "Come on Albert, you can do this."

Captain Stubbs could feel the tension as the men struggled to hold their nerve, some more noticeably than others. He looked above him, where the bright, morning sunshine was now lighting an azure blue, cloudless heaven. Tomlinson was whimpering, a terrible, ominous, pitiable sound. Fred quivered, his heart racing, thumping in his chest as the last seconds ticked away.

"Men..." Stubbs began chanting in a measured tone that belied his jangling nerves, "remember - do not run, do not stop for the wounded, and for God's sake, stay apart."

"Sorry about your tea Harold," whispered Albert.

"Don't worry mate," Harold patted his shoulder. "It's only tea. Good luck Bert."

"Good luck Harold," came the answering echo.

As Sergeant Prosser was making a last check of the ladders, seeing they were all secured, a whistle blew. It was followed swiftly by a series of whistles sounding all along the trench, as if a steam train had begun racing suddenly to its destination.

"Bloody hell Sir, Get us going!" yelled Jacko, his voice crazy with fear.

Captain Stubbs blew the whistle, "Ready men, " he shouted and blew the whistle again. "Let's go" he shouted again "Over the top men, follow me." He rose above the parapet and walked into no mans land. Prosser bawled immediately, "Go, go, go – NOW!" As Stubbs and Prosser led, suddenly all was confusion as a great wave of khaki surged up out of the trench and poured like a tide over the parapet.

Tommy Fisher, Harold Braithwaite Albert Tomlinson, Jacko Wilks, Jabez Hulse and Bill Gibson were in no mans land. In the distance, machine guns rattled, and a smoky fog was descending over the featureless expanse of mud. Bill watched Fred a few feet away as they walked steadily forward, "All right mate?

"Yeah," called Fred, "I'm all right."

---

"This isn't too bad," said Harold almost jovially, "like a walk in the park."

"The artillery lads must have done a good job, sorted them Huns out." said Prosser. The next second there was a whizzing sound. Harold dropped to his knees then fell face forward into the mud.

"Bastard sniper!" cursed Prosser.

"Harold!" Albert ran towards his friend

"Stay in line Tomlinson," warned Prosser, "keep moving, and stay low -" Sergeant Prosser had barely finished giving the order before he too fell. Staring in horror at the two motionless bodies, Fred then felt a tug on his arm as Bill urged him forward.

From the German lines an artillery bombardment was building up, and shells were bursting all around them, to the accompaniment of further sniper fire. Amid the cacophony of ceaseless noise, Bill saw men being hit on either side of him. His mouth dry with the smoke and terror, still he moved forward, there was no other way. Each time a soldier fell, the gap would close, and the inexorable march continue. Albert was sobbing as he moved, Jacko now the one forcing him to carry on.

All of them could hear the dreadful cries of the injured, some howling, calling out for a stretcher-bearer, or praying aloud. Bill, ignoring the standing orders had broken into a run now, weaving his body this way and that as the instruments of death flew around him. Fred was at his side, the two of them running towards the enemy, running towards life or death.

Still ahead, Captain Stubbs, firing his pistol had almost disappeared in the smoke. Some of the lads had died within the first few minutes; others, blown apart as the shells crashed down.
But Bill kept going, running blindly forward as the bullets whizzed passed his head - was the next one for him. Fred was still behind him.

"Keep going Bill," Tommy had appeared at his side. "Keep going."
Bill felt Tommy guiding him on and he and Fred began to run with him. Suddenly Tommy dropped into the mud. Bill dropped to his knees, took hold of Tommy's body.

"Help me Bill," he groaned.

"Give me a hand Fred," Fred and Bill lifted Tommy to his feet, but Tommy screamed in agony and fell into the mud again. Bill saw a gaping wound in his stomach.

"I can't do it Bill," Tommy pleaded, "Leave me, you've got to go."

Bill shook his head, "No...No.... Stretcher bearer" he shouted, "Stretcher bearer."

But no one came, the confusion and chaos, still in full force. The acrid smoke and the stench of blood lingered in the air. Men still ran towards the savage guns, falling as each bullet found its mark and took its cold exacting revenge.

Bill took from his backpack some bandages and held them on the stomach wound.

"Hold this on the wound Fred." But Fred didn't move. "Fred!" shouted Bill again, "Hold this." He grabbed the back of Fred's tunic and pulled him forward.

Out of the smoke Bill saw a young soldier running towards him, he didn't recognise him.

"Help us mate." He shouted to the young man. Momentarily the young man stopped. Bill saw a strange sad look in the young man's eyes.

"I can't help you" he shouted and carried on running.

"You're wasting your time with him Bill, he's lost it." Jabez Hulse knelt beside him. "Bloody coward."

Bill watched the man running back toward the trench. Suddenly he dropped to his knees, and fell forward to the ground. He was dead, shot by a snipers bullet.

"Hold this." Jabez thrust his kit bag into Bill's hands, opened it and took out more bandages. The blood soaked ones he discarded and placed the clean ones on the wound. Tommy, his eyes wide, now lay silent.

"We've got to leave him now." Jabez said, "They'll pick him up later on. Come on Bill, you too Fred, keep your heads down now." He moved off into the mist.

Fred and Bill moved forward, crouching low, running slowly on. Ahead of them he could see the fire coming from the machine guns, they were nearing the German trench...The noise was deafening and frenzied, shells fell with such ferocious rapidity, the earth was a melee of shell holes and disarray.

"Keep going Fred," he shouted to the young man, "Nearly there now, follow me."

Suddenly above, a shell was falling, breaking overhead sending its lethal shards of metal crashing to earth. The explosion ripped into the earth.

Bill lay motionless, time had stopped; all lay still in the silence. Then with rushing violence the deafening destruction surged again. He tried to climb out of the shell hole but his right leg wouldn't move, he looked down, there was a gaping hole in his thigh

"Fred" he shouted, "Fred," but he was nowhere to be seen; Fred had gone.

# CHAPTER TEN

The Somme Valley
1st July 1916
Field Hospital near the Front Line

One after another the ambulances rushed through the open gates of the field hospital a few miles from the front line. Immediately the tailgates of the lorries opened and soldiers pulled out stretchers of wounded men and laid them out for the doctors" preliminary examinations. Then the wagons roared away to fetch more casualties.

Army Nurse Jessie Turnbull and Volunteer Nurse Florrie Davis had been on shift since 4am. As Florrie was a new recruit she had been assigned to Jessie for training. Florrie quickly followed Jessie along the lines as the doctors decided who should be treated and who should be left.

One of the wounded men caught Florrie's hand.

"Help me," he gasped, "Water Miss,"

She knelt down at his side; the blood soaked bandages covered a deep open wound in the young man's stomach. He grabbed her hand tightly. Florrie began to panic.

"Nurse Davis," Jessie said sternly, "Come over here."

"Water Miss," the soldier pleaded with her, "Give me some."

Florrie prised her hand free. "I'm sorry," she said,

Two stretcher-bearers pushed her to one side "Move out of the way Miss," one of them said urgently. They picked up the young soldier laid him on a stretcher and quickly took him away. Florrie was stunned, stood immobile, unable to move, she had not seen this much chaos, and the wounded just kept on coming in.

"Nurse Davis" Jessie shouted and beckoned her to come to her side.

Florrie ran to her, her hands shook. "I can't do this Jess." She whispered. The doctor momentarily turned towards Florrie. "You are no use to me or these men if you can't do the job,"

"Just a few nerves," she replied,

The doctor looked from Jessie to Florrie then continued along his line of wounded. Finally he turned to Jessie, "These men are for surgery; the rest, the stretcher bearers deal with."

Jessie nodded, and the doctor left her and Florrie together.

"Where are the other's going Jess?"

Jessie shook her head, "Florrie, there's no hope for them, the other nurses will make them comfortable. Now we've got work to do."

Florrie began to cry. Jessie put her arm around the girl. "Come on now Florrie, you'll get used to it."

She shrugged off Jessie's arm "Get used to it…Get used to it! How can you say that, those poor lads, blown to bits and we can only watch them die! Get used to it. I'll never do that." She began to retch.

The nurse hurrying by them stared at the two women. "Matron's on her way, " she said, "Get her out of here or else she'll be for it…"

"Did you hear that Florrie?" Jessie was slowly losing her patience with the girl. "Now get a move on or go pack your bags and go." Jessie turned towards the wards.

Florrie wiped here eyes and was about to follow her when Matron turned the corner. She looked at the young nurse. "Are you alright nurse," she asked Florrie,

"I don't…. don't." she sniffed her tears back.

Just at that moment Jessie appeared at her side. "There you are Nurse," she said guiding her towards the ward, "She's got the snivels Matron, she'll be fine."

For hours Jessie, Florrie and the other nurses, their aprons covered in the soldiers' blood, tended the injured. A production line of makeshift bandaging, cleaning, treating the wounds of the endless stream of men flooding into the ward;

Jessie kept a keen eye on her charge. The young girl had settled down and was tending to the men in her care. She smiled and turned to her next patient. Removing the blooded bandages from his right thigh she saw the gaping hole. The soldier winced and grabbed his leg.

"Sorry, but I have to see what's wrong." She looked at him. His face was muddy, only his eyes were bright. His uniform covered in dirt and ragged and his boots were ripped to shreds.

"I know Miss, it hurts though."

"What happened to you?" she asked.

"Blown up Miss, shell exploded next to me, woke up in a shell hole. I was with Fred; don't know what happened to him. Hope he made it. Suppose I was lucky."

———

Jessie smiled, "Very," she said, and carefully cleaned the wound. "You'll be going down to surgery soon so I'll bandage this up for now."

The young man smiled, "Thank You Miss." He said gratefully. Jessie began to bandage the wound and was about to leave him when he took her arm.

"Can you find out what happened to a mate of mine," he asked, "He'd been shot and I had to leave him Miss,"

"There are so many…I don't know if…."

The young man's grip tightened. "Please Miss, Please." he urged, "I have to know what's happened to him."

Jessie looked at the young man's grubby face; tears were falling from his frightened eyes. She smiled, "I'll see what I can do for you, what's his name?"

The young man relaxed, "Tommy Fisher Miss,"

"And what's yours, so I can tell him who was asking after him."

"Tell him its Bill, Bill Gibson."


Eight hours later Jessie Turnbull sat down at the table in the rest room of the nurses' quarters. She was exhausted. The casualties had not stopped but she and Florrie had been relieved for two hours. Removing the blood soaked apron and sleeves she put them into the laundry pile. She poured herself a cup of tea from the freshly brewed pot and drank the warm brown liquid gratefully.

The door opened and Florrie rushed in to the sink. She retched violently then sat down on the chair opposite Jessie.

"Still they come Jess; still they come. Those poor boys." She shook her head.

Jessie moved to the stove, picked up the teapot, poured the stewing tea into a tin mug and placed it in front Florrie.

"You're doing well Florrie, keep going, just keep going, think of the soldiers, how you're helping them."

Florrie sipped the hot liquid and replaced the mug onto the table.

"But so many die Jess," she said, "Long before they get to the operating theatre, so many of them just die. I wish to God I was away from here."

Jessie smiled, "I will be in a couple of hours. After this I'm going to pack."

"Pack!" Florrie exclaimed, "Where are you going?

"Matron came to see me; I've got my orders to go back to the hospital in the city, to help the men with trench fever. The ones in charge said I've seen enough of this bloodshed, they think it might affect my thinking and they are right."

"How long have you been here?"

"I joined up in 1914 at the out break war. Been over here ever since. How long have you been here?"

"Three weeks… three bloody weeks." Florrie swore, " I can't stand it any longer. How do you cope with it, I can't sleep, daren't sleep – the nightmares." She grabbed her head.

"It's the same for me Florrie, for all of us."

"But how do we know who to treat and who to leave, they're all a mess. I don't know what to do Jess. I can't cope with it all." She sobbed heavily. "But it's just – just - not like I thought it was going to be - the noise, the constant bombings and the men howling in pain. Those poor lads, blown to bits and we can only watch them die. It's awful Jess, awful…"

Jessie put her arms around Florrie again " Now enough of this talk Florrie Davis. You'll learn to cope, you know you will, you have to for their sake. You're so young… But you'll do your best, I'm sure, as we all will. We have to look after these boys; they have no one else here."

"Oh Jess, today… I saw something so horrible…they're using maggots to clean the wounds, whatever next…."

"But it's working Florrie, that's what matters. We're saving lives, now that can't be a bad thing.

Florrie paced the room, her hands shook, "But what are we saving them for Jess? We mend their broken bodies, put them right and they send them back again. I didn't volunteer for this." She broke down in tears.

"Come and sit down Florrie," Jessie steered her to the chair again. "It's not what I signed up for. I could have stayed at home, should have stayed with Sam, looked after him. We'd have been married now." Jessie removed a locket from around her neck and opened it." She smiled at the young mans face that smiled back at her, "I'm glad he's not here. If I had known what it was like, what the trenches, the men looked and smelled like, I wouldn't be here."

Florrie wiped her eyes. "Where is Sam? My Joe's in the navy"

Jessie smiled at the photo, then closed the locket and hung it around her neck. "Sam's got a disability, his legs – fell of a horse when he was fifteen…Paralysed. At least he won't see this hellhole." Florrie squeezed her friend's hand, "I'm sorry Jess, I'm just being silly, I suppose I will get used to it."

Jessie shook her head, "No Florrie, you will never get used to this. But you will cope and do your best. You're a good nurse, that's why you're here. These men need us, rely on us. They're scared, frightened, and we can help them; show them some comfort. Just holding their hand, means more to them than you can ever know."

Florrie sighed heavily "I shall miss you Jess, you've been a good friend to me,"

Jessie hugged the young girl in a warm embrace. "If only I could take you with me, " she said, "But it will be your turn soon, a couple more months, that's all, then you'll be sent back to the hospital."

Suddenly the door burst open, a young nurse stood in the doorway. "There's more wounded coming in" she said urgently, "You're needed on the wards now."

"Here we go again," Jess smiled at Florrie and squeezed her arm. The two women shared a knowing look and rushed into the foray.

"Get some morphine," said Jessie desperately trying to hold the soldier down. "He's been in no mans land for hours"

Instantly Florrie bought the morphine and injected into his arm; almost immediately he began to settle.

"That should ease him a little." Jessie said. She reached for a glass of water from the table. She put her hand under his head and steadying him she put the glass to his mouth. The soldier drank desperately, and then lay back exhausted.

"Thank you nurse," he gasped his breath coming in short quick gasps. "My pocket, my pocket." He grabbed at his tunic pocket.

Florrie moved his hand and unbuttoned the flap "Let me" she said, and gave him the photo she had removed from it.

The soldier gave a painful smile and held the photo to her. "Tell her Miss," he gasped, "promise me you'll tell her" he coughed deeply; blood oozed from his mouth. Florrie took a wet flannel and gently wiped away the blood. He coughed again, "Tell her I love her Miss."

Florrie took the photo from the young man and held his hand in hers. "I will," she said as tears fell from her eyes. I will." She turned to Jessie, "Help me Jess, please." She whispered.

Jessie smiled, "You're doing fine, keep talking to him, just talk to him."

"He's not going to make it Jess, he's not going to make it." She shook her head.

"I'm sorry Miss," the soldier was gasping heavily, "didn't want to cause you this upset. Please tell her, my Maggie. I love her Miss; tell her I'm sorry. I was going to marry her when I got back." He began to cry and clung on to Florrie "I don't want to die Miss, I'm sorry, tell Mother and Dad I love them. I'm sorry Miss., sorry…"

Suddenly his body writhed, his eyes, full of fear widened as took one final gasp for breath, and his lifeless body sank back into the bed.

"Oh God Jess, he's gone." Florrie sobbed, "What a waste of life. So young - so innocent."

Jessie closed the young man's eyes then pulled the bed sheet over the soldiers face.

"Come on now. He's at peace." She guided Florrie away towards the table in the middle of the ward. Florrie looked at the photograph she still held. "I've got to tell her Jess, I promised him."

"May be you could write to his family, I'm sure they would like to know that you were with him when he…"

Florrie wiped her eyes. "I'll do that Jess, I'll find out his address and write to them. I'll tell them how brave he was, how he thought of them."

"What was his name?"

"I don't know," Florrie saw a brown envelop at the bottom of the bed. "Here's his paper." She opened the envelope and searched for a name. "Here it is Jess. Tommy Fisher that's him, Tommy Fisher."

Jessie had packed her belongings, and said her goodbyes. She looked at her watch, half an hour before she boarded the transport to take her to the hospital in the town.

"Enough time." she whispered, there was one place she had to go to before she left, to keep a promise she had made to young soldier in her charge. Fastening the cloak around her shoulders she headed back into the wards to find Bill Gibson.

## Sunday 11<sup>th</sup> November 1973

"You know Beattie, letters were very special to us," said Bill "they were always weeks old before we got them but we didn't care. We'd queue up when the post arrived, the sergeant would hand them out and each one of us would find a quiet corner, or some niche dug in the side of the trench, or just sit on sandbags to read them. It was our private moment. As you opened the envelope the expectation of news from home was exhilarating. Your family remembered you, loved you. It meant you still had a life outside of that hellhole, something to cling on to in those dark days. That was a good feeling. It's what you wanted to hear, gave you comfort, some promise of normality to the dreadful uncertainty we were living in. Not all the letters were good news though as is expected, but most of the time they were just what we needed.

"What do you mean not good news? Who would send a letter like that?"

Bill smiled, "Wives, girlfriends, who'd found their freedom and gone off with other men. News of brothers; sons, fathers who'd been killed…. you didn't want to get one of these."

"No you wouldn't," said Beattie sadly, "you couldn't do a thing about it, you'd be helpless."

"Even our letters home, censored or not, meant a lot to our families; we were still alive, giving them some small morsel of hope that we just might come back." Said Bill.

"A bit of a cheek censoring them. Why did they do that? Its not like any of you were going to say anything out of turn."

"They couldn't take that chance Beattie, the officers read them all and crossed out anything that didn't suit. But some officers let anything thorough, they didn't care what was written and wanted the families to know just what was happening out there."

"Well good for them I say," said Beattie vehemently, "The folks at home should have known what their men folk were going through."

---

Bill gave a wry smile. "It didn't matter, made no difference, no-one could have changed what was happening, the war still carried on. I was out of it for a while and I received one of Mothers letters when I was in hospital. She didn't know what had happened to me and I wasn't going to tell her, she'd find out soon enough. It was lovely to hear from her, telling me about home. She said our Elsie was working in the sewing factory, doing twelve-hour shifts, and Dad was helping Mr Haughton, *'Don't worry our Bill, Mr Haughton's keeping your job for you, Dad's just filling in while you're away.'*

In my minds eye I could see the farm, and the meadow, which led, down to the river. I remember smiling at the thought of Dad working there, and wishing I could have been with all of them. Then I thought of Dolly and Bess again. I hoped they were all right, but having seen what had happened to the horses, I'm sure they wouldn't be. The war had got nothing to do with them, but we put them through it, worked them to death. "

"Some came back though Bill, didn't they" Beattie said,
Bill nodded, "Only the young ones, the fittest…the others, well…" he shook his head, "They were shot or went for meat, it was awful, those poor creatures, worked their hearts out for us and that's how we treated them."

He tapped his pipe on the grate, filled it again and relit it.
"I remember Mother writing *'the whole town's talking about Nancy and Ernie, Bill. Everyone knows they're married.'* You know what people are like Beattie. Some folk said he only married her to get out of going into the army but when he volunteered a good few were surprised. Some still said he was running away from her." Bill smiled thoughtfully, "But I knew different. I saw the look in Ernie's eyes that last night in the trench. He loved her; it was obvious to see. When he spoke her name, his face lit up, but as those big guns blasted into the night sky, the realisation of where we were sank in…"

Bill paused for a moment reflecting on the memories. "Yes, we liked our letters from home. But there were some letters, official letters, sent in brown envelopes that no one wanted to receive.

# CHAPTER ELEVEN

August 1916

"It's been busy for a Wednesday morning, more like pay day," said George Burrows, smiling approvingly as two more women entered the shop and joined the line at the counter.

As proprietor of Burrows Tripe Shop, which had been selling tripe on the corner of the High Street and St George's Terrace for as long as anyone could remember, he paid close attention to the ebbs and flows of trade; the quiet days, the busy days, the days when the till groaned that he wished he had all year round, and the forlorn days when, often for no particular reason, hardly a soul put their face round the door.

"Yes," agreed Nancy pushing back her hair with the back of her hand, "I'm glad it's half day closing."

"You'll be going nowhere until you've finished serving these good folk." George laughed heartily as he said this, but he knew Nancy often liked to slip off on the stroke of one on a half day. She was popular with the customers, even the ones that gossiped about her behind her back, and George always liked to keep his customers happy.

It had occurred to him – and this made him feel slightly guilty, as if he was employing a fairground freak to draw in trade - that some of them just liked to come in to gawp at Nancy, especially the older women that remembered her mother, the infamous 'scarlet woman' of the village. Now that was a story, a sad one in many ways, but Nancy seemed happy enough, despite the not always discreet snide remarks. And it wasn't easy for any woman whose husband was in the army these days he reflected, they must always be on edge. George thanked his lucky stars he was too old to fight, but he felt sorry for the poor blighters copping it out in France.
Nancy returned the laugh. She put her hands boldly on her ample hips and played to the queue, "He's a right slave driver this one you know, I've a good mind to tell him so too."

"I think you just did love," grinned Mrs. Roberts, placing her purchase in her wicker basket.

"I did didn't I!" said Nancy archly. "Now who's next?"

A moment later Nancy noticed Mary King lingering outside the shop. Nancy glanced at Mr Burrows, who gave her a brief nod. She then wrapped six sausages and two large pieces of tripe in brown paper, tied it with white string and placed it under the counter. When Mary reached the counter Nancy reached down and handed her the parcel.

"Here's your tripe Mrs King, and we've just got some eggs in fresh today." Nancy packed half a dozen eggs into a paper bag.

Mary tipped the contents of her purse out into the palm of her hand: there were just two small copper coins. Staring at them she said very quietly, "I'll just take the tripe please if you don't mind."

Nancy lowered her eyes. The sadness in Mary's voice, in her eyes as she continued staring at the two little coins, was too much. Nancy turned to look at her employer.

"I'll put it on the slate Mary, don't you worry about it lass" he smiled magnanimously.

"I don't want charity Mr. Burrows."

"And I'm not giving you any. Like I said, I'll put it on the slate."

Mary looked at Nancy, smiled wanly and took the package and the brown paper bag. "Next week Mr. Burrows, next week, I'll have the money then."

"Settle up when you can. Now get yourself off home, them thunder clouds have been threatening rain and you've little un's to feed."

Mary King's voice trembled as she spoke, "Thank you."

The bell above the door tinkled and she was gone.

"Poor woman," said Nancy, "It must be so hard for her to manage with three children now Percy's gone." She turned to Mr. Burrows, "It's good of you to help her out."

"The least a decent man can do is to assist within the community in time of need," said George with a dignified air. His features then wrinkled and he slammed a meat cleaver down loudly on the chopping block. "This blasted war, I wish it was over."

"So do we all," Nancy sighed, and began tidying the counter.

As George bent over the till to sort the day's takings he said, "Leave that to me, you'd best be off now, its past one o" clock."

"I'm not in any hurry," replied Nancy.

"I never said you were, it's just that I'm sure you've things of your own to do."

Nancy stopped what she was doing and straightened up. "Mr. Burrows, do you mind if I ask you a question?"

"By all means, but if its about Saturday afternoon I'm afraid I will need you all day, its no good trying to make up a little extra time now because - "

"You think that's why I'm hanging around?"

"No, no, I didn't mean – I just didn't want there to be any misunderstanding that's all. After all you do normally rush off on the dot."

"To mope over that 'that absurdly young man' of mine – yes I've heard what people say."

George coughed and began carefully counting a pile of pennies. "I don't know what you mean, your private life's your own affair my dear."

"Not round here," replied Nancy meaningfully.

George snapped the till shut. "Now what's brought this on Nancy?" he said, "not like you to get a chip on your shoulder about something."

"I know what folk say – that I'm too old for Ernie, that he's too good for me, that I was glad to have anyone take me on. Oh yes, I've heard the whispers – and they're not always whispers! Well I'm nothing like my mother, nothing. But her legacy lingers, I've been haunted by it all my life."

"Now then girl don't take on so," chided George, "don't listen to them old gossips, what do they know?"

"They know all about what happened, how my mother left me and ran off with that farm hand. *'Granny reared that one,'* I've heard the so-called good Christian folk whispering in the middle pews of the church, while we have to sit in the draughty ones at the back." Looking at George intently now she said, "You knew my mother didn't you – tell me honestly, what was she really like?"

George leaned back against the counter, folded his arms and looked thoughtful for a moment. "I won't beat about the bush Nancy, your mother was a beauty, and she knew it. Her fair locks and them soulful lilac blue eyes could fetch ducks off water. And oh how she liked to be admired! There was plenty of Fellas' 'round here as used to pander to her charms. Do anything to win a smile from her."

"Its true then," said Nancy, "Granny sent her into service to keep her out of trouble. But trouble seemed to find her and she come back home with more than she went with."

They both laughed. "Look on the bright side, you were the best thing that happened to your Granny," said George, "gave her a purpose in life again."

"I suppose so," Nancy said.

"And remember this," said George, "your mother could have given you up for adoption to a stranger, that's what most girls that got in trouble did. But she loved you, never be in any doubt of that."

"Oh I know, at least, I think I know," Nancy's voice trembled slightly.

"Be in no doubt of it. But your granny wanted to bring you up, and your mother accepted that was what was best for you, she being a woman on her own like. But it was your mother that paid to make sure you were always well fed and clothed and sent to school. Your grandma may have given you a roof, but your mother provided the bread and butter, and the jam."

Nancy stared in surprise, "She paid for my food, but how did she find the money if she was working in service?"

George said gently, "I think you know the answer to that as well as I do."

"Yes," said Nancy quietly.

"She got the extra money the only way she knew how. People said she had no pride, but she had more than pride. She loved you. "

"I know, I know," repeated Nancy, the beginnings of tears in her eyes now. "But still she left me. Knowing why doesn't make it easier. And all my life I've had it drilled into me by my grandmother that I must never bring any further shame on the family. Believe me I hope I never have and never will. But I've heard what people say: *'The apple never falls far from the tree.'* I'll admit I've courted a few lads, but none of them came up to my Ernie. They said he married me to avoid going to war, and that that backfired on him when conscription came in. But none of it's true, he didn't marry me because of that."

"I know that," agreed George, "you'd been walking out for some time if I remember rightly."

---

104

"We tried to keep it quiet, away from them gossips. I knew he was right for me when he come flying round the corner on his bike and knocked me over on me back. He helped me up, dusted me down and said 'Sorry love!' with a big soft grin all over his face. For a moment, just for a moment, we looked at each other. 'Can I walk out with you,' he said, 'Sunday next, that's if you're not busy.' 'I'm not busy.' I said. 'Then I'll see you Sunday my lady.' He was whistling as he pedalled off down the road, looking back and smiling just before he rounded the bend. That's when I knew he was going to be mine."

George Burrows smiled. "So did I Nancy," he said, "you never shut up about him. He's a good man, lass."

Nancy nodded. "Yes he is, treats me like a lady he does. Calls me his sweetheart; all that bluster and bragging, he means none of it you know."

"He's just young and daft with it," said George. "But his heart's in the right place, that's all that matters."

"I didn't want him to go to war, but I always knew he would. I could see the sadness in his eyes when he saw the boys that joined up that recruiting day, those fine young men, all full of hope, and innocence. Then some of them coming back, blinded, some without limbs, all of them broke into a thousand pieces inside."

There was silence for a moment then George said, "Ernie will be alright you know, he leads a charmed life and he's got you waiting for him when he comes home. Any man would be proud to have you as his wife, he'll let no one take that away from him."

Nancy came over and kissed his cheek, "Thank you Mr Burrows, I do love him you know. And I love you too – that is, I mean, as a -" she hesitated.

"Kindly uncle?" suggested George.

"If you'll accept the title."

"With pleasure," said George.

The shop bell tinkled and a middle-aged woman came in.

"Hello Mrs Gibson," said Nancy.

"I know its half day, but are you still open?" enquired Mrs Gibson hopefully.

"Officially we closed at one. Unofficially, what can I get you? You get off home Nancy -"

"No, no, that's all right," insisted Nancy, "is it your usual Mrs. Gibson?"

"Yes please love, but can I have three pieces this time, our Bertha's coming over, so she'll want feeding. Tripe and onions usually goes down a treat with her."

Nancy wrapped the goods and handed them to Mrs Gibson. "Have you heard from your Bill?" she asked.

"A letter came this morning as a matter of fact, not much in it really, he's not one for writing. He says they're doing all right though. What about your Ernie?"

Nancy shook her head, "Nothing yet, but the post's been delayed where he is apparently, so maybe his letter is on it's way."

Mrs Gibson bid them good day and headed for the door just as Sam Hawks the postman, a letter in his hand, breezed in. He handed Nancy the letter. "Save me a walk up the hill Nance - looks like it's from Ern."

Nancy's eyes had lit up. She took the letter with a grateful smile and tucked it immediately into a pocket beneath her apron.

Sam lingered, curious, "Aren't you going to read it?"

"Thanks Sam, I'll read it in a minute. I'll let you know how he is."

"Give the girl some privacy lad," George said, "Go on get yourself home now Nancy. And thanks for staying on to serve Mrs Gibson. I'll make it up to you."

She untied her apron and folded it into a neat bundle. Taking her summer coat and straw boater from behind the counter she put on both, fixing the boater to her strawberry blonde curls with a long silver hatpin. "See you tomorrow," she smiled, and closed the shop door.

It had just begun to rain as Nancy turned the corner into St George's Road. She turned up her collar and made her way quickly along the pavement towards her house.

"Hey up Nance, you heard from Ernie yet?" asked Jacob Groves the coalman from the top of his cart as he brought his horse to a stop beside her.

Nancy beamed proudly, "Got a letter today Jacob, going to read it when I get in."

"He must be all right then," said the coalman, "they'll be coming home soon, you'll see."

"Yes, let's pray for that."

Suddenly it seemed to Nancy as if everyone in the village was being nice to her; no sideways glances, and not a whispered remark all morning. Perhaps she read too much into people's behaviour. Whatever, it must be a good omen she thought.

Jacob bid her good day and flicked the reins gently across the horse's back. The animal's tail swished back and forth as if swatting a fly, and the hooves resumed their rhythmic clip clop along the cobblestones.

As she approached her house, Nancy saw a small crowd gathered by the village hall further along the street. Passing her house by she continued on towards them. Getting nearer she realised they were studying the notice board. Suddenly a young woman screamed, "Oh God no, he's on the list, oh God, he's on the list!" She pushed past Nancy and ran off in the other direction.

Nancy then felt a tap on her shoulder and turned to see her neighbour Joan Dakin. "You'd better go to Lily," Joan said solemnly, "It's Stanley, she's had the telegram."

Nancy heard the dreadful crying even before she reached her friend's house. She pushed the door and went in. The crying was louder, interspersed with screams of 'Why, why?' Nancy entered the kitchen, where Lily Jenkins stood by the black kitchen grate rocking her young baby daughter in her arms, sobbing and calling Stanley's name. The three older children, Jonno, Reg and Phoebe, were sitting together, still and silent on the small tattered couch by the window.

"Oh, Lily, I'm so very sorry my love, give her here," said Nancy. She took the baby gently from her friend and placed her in the wooden cot resting by the grate. Then Nancy put her arms around her friend and held her close. Lily sobbed; her heart rending cries resonating through the house.

"What am I going to do?" she wailed, "I told him not to go. We need him here with us. I can't manage without him. I miss him. Oh God I can't carry on." Wracked with despair she pushed Nancy away and grabbed Reg and Phoebe from the couch. "Here," she said thrusting them towards Nancy, "take them, you have them, please, I can't send them away to that workhouse, 'cos that's where we're going to end up now." The two children ran to Nancy and buried their heads in her long skirt, while at the same time reaching out their arms to their mother. Lily almost fell onto the couch. Jonno, the eldest child put his arms around her.

"You're not going there," Nancy said decisively. "Think about your children"

Through reddened tear-filled eyes Lily stared at her friend. "But I am thinking about them, I can't go on Nancy, I've no food, no money, and there's nothing coming from the army. I don't know what to do."

"You could always come and stay with me, for a while, till you get on your feet again. There's the spare room, it'll be a bit cramped but we'll muddle through I'm sure."

"I want to stay here Nancy," she sobbed, "It's our home."
From the hallway appeared Mrs Edgerton. "She's coming home with me, where she belongs. Come on Lily, get yourself together." She spoke harshly to her daughter.

"Mother I can't do that," protested Lily, "there's not room for us all."

"There's plenty of room at the farm, now come on, get yourself ready. Take only what you can carry, your father and a couple of the lads will come for the rest tomorrow."

"No, they're my children," said Lily, breathing heavily but a little calmer now. "I can't take them out of their home."

"If you'd have listened to us in the first place you would have been taken care of," snapped Mrs Edgerton.

At this last remark Lily fled from the room and up the stairs, her footsteps sounding on the floorboards as she ran into the bedroom. Nancy turned to follow her but Mrs Edgerton grabbed her arm. "Leave her be," she said firmly, "help me with the children."
The two boys and little Phoebe bemused by the chaos sat in fearful silence on the couch, not daring to move now that Granny Edgerton had arrived. Little Gwen began crying again, Jonno picked her up and held her tightly.

"Jonno, put her back in the cot and get yourselves ready, you're coming to the farm," said Mrs. Edgerton. "I don't know Nancy," she continued, shaking her head, "if only Stanley had listened to us, he'd still be here.

"What do you mean?" asked Nancy.

"We wanted him to come and work on the farm, they could have all come and lived with us, yes it would have been crowded what with all this lot and the rest of the family, but we'd have managed. Lily wanted to come home, I know she did, but Stanley, oh no not him, wanted to make his own way he said. Always was pig headed, the stubborn fool."

Nancy was not sure how to respond to this. Lily had just lost her husband and was upstairs distraught. Was this any way for her mother to behave? She felt the most acute pity for her friend, and was incensed at Mrs Edgerton's unkind words. "He looked after his family well enough," she said, trying to control her anger.

"I didn't want her to marry him," continued Mrs Edgerton in the same carping tone, "but she wouldn't listen to me, he'd won her over with his fine talk and promises, and landed her with this lot." Mrs Edgerton nodded to the children, "how many more would she have had if -"

"Them are cruel words Mrs Edgerton," interrupted Nancy, "Stanley was a good man."

"I'm not saying he was a bad man -"

"It sounds very like that to me -"

"Shut up! Shut up! Stop saying nasty things about my dad!" Jonno yelled. "He's dead! He's not coming home!" As he began to scream loudly Reg and Phoebe huddled close to him, they were all crying now.

Suddenly Lily ran back down the stairs and the door flew open. "What's going on, what have you said Mother?" she demanded angrily.

"Only the truth Lily, now for the last time get yourself ready, you're coming home."

Lily took little Gwen from Jonno's arms and stood beside her children. "No Mother we are not. We'll stay here, I'll manage."

Gertrude Edgerton leaned menacingly towards her daughter, "If you've no money my girl, you can't pay the rent. You'll be out on your ear and up before the courts for debt as like."

Lily turned to her friend. "Please, Nancy, you understand, I can't leave here, its Stan's home, our home. When you've got children of your own you'll understand."

Nancy looked around the sparsely furnished, shabby room. She had to admit it this was no place to bring up those children. She put her hand on her friend's shoulder. "Come on Lily," she said kindly, "there's nothing here for you now. I'll help you pack."

The August sunshine was breaking through the dispersing rain clouds as Mrs Edgerton, Lily and her brood left the house that had been the only home the children had known. Nancy held her friend in a tight embrace.

"I'm so very sorry," said Nancy. "If there's anything you need, anything I can do, get word to me. We'll keep in touch."

"We will," whimpered Lily, "we must."

Nancy waited until they had turned the corner and were gone from sight. The image of Lily's face, grief-stricken and bereft, tore at her heart. At least they wouldn't starve on the farm, was all she could think. But the idea of her friend being under the perpetual carping tongue of her mother Gertrude Edgerton was painful to contemplate. What choice did she have though? Perhaps in a while we can come up with another solution, thought Nancy. Lily and the children deserved better than living under a dictatorship, for Stan's memory as well as for themselves.

Crossing the road to her own home Nancy opened the door, hung her coat and hat in the hall and went to the kitchen. She took Ernie's precious letter from her pocket. His handwriting hasn't improved, she said to herself with a smile as she read the scrawled address on the envelope. But that scrawl was for her the most beautiful thing she had ever seen, and now she wanted everything perfect before she sat down to savour what was inside.

She lit a candle and placed it on the windowsill. "There, that's nice isn't it Ern?" she said aloud. Filling the kettle she placed it on the grate and lit the fire she had laid that morning. Now she could sit down. She opened the envelope and took out the letter, holding it first to her cheek and breathing its aroma, stroking the paper against her cheek. So strange to think how many miles it had travelled, and over what terrain! And it had begun life with her beloved husband taking up his pen and pressing it to the page, dedicating his words intimately to her, speaking to her and her alone…. she began to read:

*My Dearest Nancy*

*We've all arrived in this other place now; can't tell you where it is, but it's different than where we've been before; there seems a lot of us here. Think this might be a big one. Anyway I'll get through it like I have done, and then I'll be back home soon with you. When I get out of this lot I'll find a job and I can tell you, it won't be selling papers. It'll be a proper job with good prospects and good wages…. then we can start our own family like we've talked about. You've got my army pay and that should keep you going. Nancy, you're not to worry about me, I'll be alright. But whatever happens, always know that I love you so very much. I've never regretted one moment with you, you make me so happy.*

*All my love Ernie.*

With tears pricking her eyes Nancy rose from the table and took her wedding photograph from the sideboard. Holding the image close she gazed into her husband's eyes. "Can't tell me where you are eh!" she said, half laughing, half crying with the outpouring of love his simple words had stirred in her. "Ah but I've got a good idea, I've been reading them newspapers you know." She wagged her finger playfully at him.

111

"The big push they're calling it, and you'll be mixed up in it somehow I'm sure! I do miss you Ernie, I light the candle, just like I said I would. You'll see it and know I'm waiting for you. I remember what you said: "A light in the darkness" and then you held me in your arms and kissed me ever so tenderly and promised me you'd come back."

She replaced the photograph and walked to the window. The street was quiet now, the crowd from the village hall dispersed, only a pair of elderly neighbours passing by Lily's former home opposite. Nancy wondered what would happen to it now. Where once there had been love, there was now emptiness, the happy voices of the children no longer rang out, the heart of a family had been torn out and was gone forever. Time heals they said, but how could it heal this? Ernie's loving words caressed her heart. I am the luckiest person alive, she thought. It's unfair, so unfair, poor Lily.

At that moment a moving shape caught Nancy's attention. A boy was cycling down the street, glancing from one side to the other. He must be looking for a house number she thought; odds or evens, she said to herself. The boy slowed and looked in her direction. Nancy saw him taking something from a satchel, was it a letter - or a telegram? She felt her throat suddenly tighten. Nancy looked away from the window. Holding her breath she began counting, one, two three four…

The knock when it came was quite quiet, a tap almost. She did not move, it was obviously a mistake, he wanted to ask directions, or probably a bailiff's notice for Stan, he had always been getting into debt, well she would tell the boy she had never heard of the family, one less thing for Lily to worry about. The knock came again, louder this time.

The journey to the door seemed an eternity. Nancy opened it. The boy stood to attention in his smart uniform. He said her name and she nodded then signed the piece of paper he held out to her. Behind the closed door she opened the telegram with shaking hands.

*Dear Mrs Fowles.*
*It is with the deepest regret that I have to inform you that your husband Private Ernest Fowles was killed in action on 1ˢᵗ of July 1916. He was in the first wave of the offensive, which started at 7.30am on that day. He fought well and carried out his duty…*

Nancy sat at the table as in a dream. By the flickering candle she read Ernie's letter again. She wiped away her tears and walked to the window. With one gentle blow, the flame, like Ernie's life, was gone. Outside the clouds had gathered once more.

## Sunday 11ᵗʰ November 1973

Beattie placed the small tray she'd brought from the kitchen on the small coffee table. She poured the brewed tea into two china cups and pushed one towards Bill.

"Put another log on the fire Bill, its nearly out. Must be all that talking we've been doing."

"You mean I've been doing" He laughed, and gently placed a couple of logs into the grate.  He took the poker and stirred the embers, immediately the fire began to reawaken.  He watched it for a moment then propped the poker against the hearth and leaned back in the chair again.

"If you want me to shut up just say so. I do ramble on sometimes when I've got someone to ramble on to." His mood had now become a bit lighter, and he sipped the tea with some relish.

"I'm surprised you want to talk about that war Bill, you've told me such a lot, much more than you've ever said before."
Bill put the cup and saucer down on the table, and stared into the fire again. "May be too much Beattie, " he said.

After a small scrap of respite from the horrors, his mood was now darkening again.

"All these years I've kept it inside, this monster, hiding it away, but sometimes, when I was off my guard, weak, vulnerable, it would creep out." He shook his head again, "Why Beattie, why did all this have to happen."

"I don't know Bill, I really don't, but if you want to get it off your chest, I'm a good listener."
Bill gave her a kindly smile then turned towards the fire to search the dancing flames for some support.

"I was in hospital for nearly four weeks after that first day on the Somme and I was glad to be there I don't mind telling you, at least I was safe from them guns.  But the guilt; it cut me up. The lads were still out there, still fighting. I didn't know how many were left. One of the nurses did tell me that Tommy Fisher had died." He took another sip of the now lukewarm tea.

"The doctors had removed most of the shrapnel in my leg and I was on the mend. I still limped but they told me that would get better with time. They never did say how much time it would take." Bill rubbed his leg; shallow empty laughter emerged from a cold, wry smile.

---

114

"Then later I was to be sent to one of the camps to recuperate before going back. I did hope they would send me back to Blightly but that was not to be. They were running short of men, so they patched you up and sent you back. I spent another two weeks there trying to walk properly and eventually they passed me as fit to go back to my battalion. I'd already packed my bag and was ready to be sent out when I got the order to report to the main barracks. I thought I was in trouble for skiving, or not getting fitter sooner, and when the captain asked me to sit down I knew that was it. But it wasn't so..... I'd been chosen to be in a line up of twelve men, a shooting party; an execution of one of our own."

# CHAPTER TWELVE

September 1916
Another Dawn is Breaking

Albert opened the door of the small wooden hut. "Drink this," he said to Bill and Jabez and set three mugs down on the table. The three men had been sent the front line on a special task.
Jabez took a long drink, "Its tea!" he exclaimed, "Where did you get it?"

"From the canteen," Albert replied. "They got sandwiches too, we can have some after we've finished here."
Bill however set his down on the bench next to him. He hand shook. Albert sat beside him. "Soon be over mate," he patted Bill's shoulder.

"Jacko's got out of this nicely, lucky bastard."

"Don't call a shattered knee cap lucky." Said Jabez, "He's in a bad way I hear."
Albert nodded, "Yeah that Gerry bayonet got him right through his leg, he did get three of 'em before they got him though."

"We got to him just in time." Jabez said, "He'd have bled to death, then…"

"Don't like it," Bill stared ahead of him, "It's not right, they shouldn't ask us to do this…I should have looked after him…"

"We were too busy looking after ourselves, it was hell out there. Jacko knew what he was doing."

"I'm talking about Fred, "said Bill angrily. "He's a kid lads, not had a life yet, and now we're taking it from him."

"So is Jacko." Jabez uttered. "At least he ran towards the Gerries – not run off and leave us to it."
Bill turned sharply, "He was looking for me!" he shouted, "I told him to follow me; he thought I was dead after that shell exploded. He didn't know where to go. You both knew that, why didn't you tell the court marshal." Bill stood up and paced the floor.

"Like you did Bill," said Albert. "And what did they do about it – ignored it and still condemned him."
Jabez shook his head. "His fate was sealed Bill when he ran the wrong way, you know that."

Bill turned on Albert and Jabez. "Then why didn't you stop him, both of you, you saw him, the state he was in; you should have stopped him."

"We tried Bill, he was crazy," Albert said. "Gotta get away," he ranted, "get away…." Then he ran away."

"He knocked me to the floor, strong little bugger." Jabez rubbed his jaw, "There was no reasoning with him."

"So it's my fault he's in there," Bill ranted, "My fault"

"No mate, it's all of us and none of us." Albert said

Jabez put his cup down and put his hand on Bill's shoulder. "Just do as they say Bill.", "We don't have a choice. Don't go answering them back and questioning them or else you'll be for it."

"Load your rifle, and fire," said Albert "Just fire,"

Bill stood up and began pacing the floor. "I don't like this," he said wringing his hands, "Killing them Germans, that's one thing…he's only a kid."

There was a shout from outside the window. "Officer approaching," Captain Stubbs opened the door carrying a bottle of brandy; the three soldiers stood, rigid to attention.

"At ease men," he said. "Get your tins ready,"

Albert and Jabez tipped the dregs from their mugs into the small sink then held out their mugs.

"Where's your tin Gibson?" Stubbs asked leaning unsteadily towards Bill. Bill could smell the unmistakable odour of brandy on the captain's breath.

"I don't want any Sir." Bill replied. "I'll just have my tea."

Captain Stubbs stared at the young man. Bill noticed the Captain's hands were shaking and his eyes red as if he had been crying. "Come on Gibson, hold out your tin. Its good French Brandy not like the rum we usually give you chaps. "

Bill refused again. "No thank you Sir I want a clear head."

Albert grabbed Bill's tin mug. "Here it is Sir, he'll drink it later."

Captain Stubbs stared at Bill, filled the mug. Then turned to leave,

"Sir," Bill said firmly. "I wish to stand down from this order."

Captain Stubbs stopped and slowly turned around. Albert and Jabez stared at Bill he stood rigid.

"No Gibson, you will obey the order." Stubbs turned, and began to walk towards the door.

"He is my friend, Sir" Bill shouted, "I can't kill him"

Captain Stubbs momentarily stopped "Obey the damned order Gibson" then he opened the door and was gone.

Jabez grabbed hold of Bill and shook him. "For god's sake Bill, do you want to get yourself killed as well - eh!"

Bill sank onto one of the camp beds. "It's my fault he's in there. My bloody fault" He began to cry again.

"It's the damn war Bill that's to blame, not you."

Albert offered Bill the tin mug. "Drink this," he said kindly, "Won't take the pain away but it'll deaden it."

Bill took the mug from Albert, stared inside at the brandy and with one gulp swallowed the liquor grimacing as the vile liquid trickled down his throat.


Fred Carter sat at the table. An oil lamp cast an amber glow across the blank writing paper. The young man took a drink of tea from the tin mug and replaced it on the table. He sighed heavily, and then took up the pen resting across the paper. In the shadows of the corner of the room sat Father Pennymore.

"What shall I write Father," Fred said, "How do I tell them?"

"Tell them how much you love them Fred," he said, his voice gentle and kind.

"But what are they going to think of me; what shame I've brought them." Fred began to sob. "I didn't do anything wrong, got lost that's all. I'm not a coward Father, not a coward as they say I am."

The reverend shook his head, and moved to the young man's side. Putting a comforting hand on his shoulder he said, "Come on now Fred, let me write it for you." He sat down at the table took up the pen and paper.

Fred stood up and paced the room, wringing his hands. "I'm frightened, Father, scared," he sobbed, " I don't want to die." He pleaded, "Oh God, I don't want to die."

Reverend Pennymore escorted Fred back to the table. "Let's write the letter Fred," he took up the pen and paper again and began to write, "Dearest Mother and Father…. he said, waiting for Fred to say more.

"What shall I tell her?" Fred asked. "The shame of it will break her heart." He stood up and paced the room. "And Dad too – it's a small village where I come from, the word will soon get round." He turned to the Reverend, "I never meant any of this Reverend, I…"

Suddenly the cell door opened, Fred immediately stood to attention as Captain Stubbs entered. "Sit down Fred," he said kindly, "I want to talk to you about what happened."

"I'm not a coward Sir, like they're saying" not me Sir."
Father Pennymore moved to the seat in the corner as Captain Stubbs sat down on the chair opposite Fred.

"Tell me again what happened Fred," he said

"You know Sir, you were there."

"I want your version Fred,"

"Yes Sir, sorry Sir. You see Bill and me, we were doing all right; then Tommy fell right next to us. We stayed with him for a bit. Bill put a bandage on his wound, and then Jabez Hulse came up and told us to carry on so we did. It was the explosion, Sir, the noise. I couldn't see, didn't know where I was. Started running but I got lost Sir, got confused, so I ran, thought I was going the right way, then I ended up back at the trench."

"You were firing your rifle at your own men?"

"I thought they were Germans Sir, I thought I'd reached their trench. Then one of the lads knocked me over, that's when I realised where I was."

"The reports say you were hysterical

"Maybe I was, I was scared that's all I know, all that noise, and the smoke, I couldn't take it Sir." Fred began to shake again.

"It's alright Fred," Captain Stubbs patted his shoulder, "Tell me how you felt when you got to the medical station."

"Better Sir, much better, no noise of them guns, no explosions. I didn't feel scared, I'd have done anything to stay there, Sir, but they sent me back."

"And two weeks later you ran away again?"

"No Sir, not this time. I didn't get out of the trench. I couldn't move; I was so scared."

"Why didn't you tell the Doctor that Fred, when we sent you back again he might have helped you."

"I wasn't ill, not like them poor lads, just my head Sir,"

There was a momentary silence; then Captain Stubbs asked, "How old are you Fred?"

"I'm seventeen now Sir," He answered. "Sixteen when I enlisted. Fooled that recruiting fella, Mum said I looked older than I was."

Captain Stubbs stood up. "Fred, tell me again why didn't you tell the Doctor how you felt the second time."

Fred smiled, "I told you, I wasn't ill, felt better when I was away from the guns. You see, it's the noise Sir." Fred put his hands over his ears. "Can't stand it."

The captain patted Fred's shoulder, went over to the reverend, shook his head and offered him the bottle of Brandy.

As he closed the door the reverend sat next to Fred, took the tin mug and poured the dregs of the tea onto the floor and filled it with the brandy.

"Get this down you son," Reverend Pennymore said offering the cup to Fred. "I'll join you" he put the bottle to his lips and drank from it. Placing the bottle down on the table he picked up the pen and notepaper again and said, "Come on Fred, let's get this letter written, Dear Mother and Father…"

Bill was restless, sleep had been elusive and the night had been long. He gazed through the window. Over the horizon the dawn light was steeling through the darkness.

He looked at Albert and Jabez; both were deep in slumber. "Come on lads" He gently shook them.

Albert rubbed his eyes. "What's up Bill?"

"Look" Bill pointed to the window, "The sun's coming up. Soon be time."

Suddenly the door opened, "Right lads," the sergeants voice rang out. "Fall in."

Bill Gibson Jabez Hulse and Albert Tomlinson took hold of their rifles, paused for a moment and walked to the parade ground.

Through the small barred window Reverend Pennymore saw the dawn's light breaking through. Fred, his head resting on his hands on the desk had fallen asleep. The padre put his hand on Fred's shoulder. The young man lifted his head.

"This is it, Reverend, isn't it" Fred said and began to weep. "The end of it all," The reverend put his arm around the young boy.

———

The cell door creaked opened; two soldiers stepped forward, tied Fred's hands behind his back and escorted him outside. Fred began to panic; they held him firm. Reverend Pennymore touched his arm, and smiled at Fred,

"Say a prayer for me Father," Fred sobbed,
The padre smiled kindly "I will Fred, I will."

Bill Gibson walked across the parade ground towards the small hut. Once inside he threw the gun down, run the cold-water tap and splashed the cool liquid over his head. He sat down at the table and run his fingers through his hair.

"That was horrible" he said to himself, "Not doing that again, poor sod." He wiped the sweat from his forehead. "Walked out as calm as anything from that cell, even smiled and nodded to us as the sergent tied him to the chair. It was only when they put the blindfold on him that he began to panic a bit, then they pinned the white cloth over his heart. *'That's the target lads,'* the sergeant said casual as you like, *'Just aim for that.'*

My hands shook as I loaded the gun, Then the Sarge said, *'Aim, Fire.'* I aimed blindly, I couldn't shoot him. But when the gunsmoke cleared he was still alive, wounded but still alive. Oh God I said I wouldn't cry." Bill wiped his eyes with the sleeve of his jacket. "Captain Stubbs saw him off, put a bullet in his head. I'm sure he was crying when he did it. It bothered me and all, - Not right this, he was only 17 - not doing that again."

As Andrew Stubbs walked away from the parade ground he could feel the tears filling his eyes. Closing the door to the officers' quarters, he walked to the side table and from the silver tray picked up the bottle of whisky and poured out a large glass full. Taking the decanter with him he sat down on one of the armchairs. He threw his cap onto the armchair opposite, placed the decanter on the small side table next to him and took a long drink from the glass.

He was grateful the room was empty; he wanted to come to terms with what he had just done. Killing hung heavy with him, he had killed, to save his life. But killing one of his own; that was unforgivable. Fred was 17 years of age, scared out of his wits and his only crime was to run the wrong way.

Refilling the glass again he took another long drink. He thought of Olivia, what would she think of him now. How could he go back to her knowing what he had done? He would live a lie; that he couldn't do; but telling her the truth…she wouldn't understand, how could she – no one would.

He poured more whisky into the glass. Tomorrow he would be back on the front line, tomorrow he would lead his men into no mans land and death would be waiting for some of them, maybe even for him,

"Only God would know" he laughed, "And would you know God if another one of those young men got lost in the dirty filthy smoke, if he were to run the wrong way, would I have to kill him.
He shook his head, "I can't do that again." He sighed heavily. "Fred trusted you God, the padre told him you'd be at his side. So where were you when the shell fell and he ran, confused, scared to death, not knowing which way was right or wrong. If you were there God, why didn't you send him towards the enemy, at least he would have died honourably."

He took another long drink of whisky. "There's no grave for him God, nothing to mark the spot where he fell. And we shot him; his mates shot him, ordered by us to do so. Who will remember him now God?" He closed his eyes and sobbed.
The door opened, "Are you alright Sir?" the sergeant asked
Andrew wiped his eyes and stood up.

"Err… Yes sergeant. Quite alright."
He straightened his tunic and picked up his cap. About to put it on he looked at the badge. It meant everything he had come to despise. He threw the cap back onto the armchair.

"Your cap Sir," the sergeant shouted after him as Andrew strode out of the room. "You'll get court marshalled if you go outside without it."
Andrew Stubbs laughed, "There will be no court marshall for me Sergeant. Not where I'm going."

From the wooded area a short distance from the camp, a single shot rang out. Captain Andrew Stubbs was dead.

## CHAPTER THIRTEEN

Ghosts
11<sup>th</sup> November 1918

Bill Gibson sat alone on the sandbags in the trench. Since first light there had been an expectation, an anticipation of an end to the conflict. The rumours had started two days ago, and unlike most rumours that got lost in translation, this one seemed to have some credibility.

"Them rumours better be right," he mused, "Heard it all before though, but it's never happened yet. Fair works me up it does, and the rest of the lads shouldn't wonder, though we none of us talk of it." He'd cleaned his gun three times already and was beginning a fourth when from further down the trench a cheer rang out. He looked at his watch, 10.50am.

"What are they cheering for?" he muttered to himself.
A young soldier Davy Sparks carrying a bottle of brandy in one hand and a tin mug in the other ran up to him.

"Hey Bill, " he shouted, "you heard this - rumour has it, this lot could be over by tonight."
Bill shook his head, "Just rumours mate; that's all."

"Supposed to be right this time, we'll be going home, seeing our families again." Davy took a swig from the bottle.
Bill seemed agitated, "Wish they'd make their bloody minds up." He said anxiously. "All morning they've been having us stand to; then standing us down. What's going on?"

From further down the trench the joyous sounds of men singing and cheering resounded. Sergeant Monks rounded the bend waving a piece of paper.

"It's over lads," he grinned, "The truce was signed the early hours of this morning. I've just received this from H.Q. --- Hostilities cease in seven minutes."
Davy slapped Bill's back, "Told you mate. Hip, hip, hurray."

"Don't do anything daft Davy, keep your head down lad, there's still snipers about. We stand down in half an hour. " Sergeant Monks walked along the trench to the next line of soldiers.
Davy took another swig of brandy. "So it is true then - Come on Bill, I'll go and get some more of this, then we can celebrate." He walked back along the trench.

"Keep your head down Davy," Bill called after him. "Still snipers about...." Bill's voice trailed off. He picked up his gun and began cleaning it again. "Bet it's not right, we'll still here. I better keep this clean just in case...."

In the distance church bells began ring out. "Not heard them for years..."

"Its over Bill," Davy carrying a another bottle of brandy, ran, with some excitement towards Bill, "Finished, the end of it." He poured out some more liquid from the bottle into his cup. "Want some?"

Bill shook his head. "No thanks Davy, you enjoy it mate."

"Come on Bill," Davy slapped Bill's shoulder, "the war's over, we won, them Gerries beaten. You heard them church bells?"

"It's right then," Bill smiled, "Over and done with."

Davy put the bottle down on the floor next to where Bill had been sitting. "That's right mate," Davy laughed still dancing round. He grabbed Bill's arms and led him around the trench with him in his euphoria, "Over and done with. Lieutenant Thomas is going to let us go into the village later. All of them mademoiselles Bill, just waiting for us..."

Bill shook his head, "Not for me mate and you've got a lass at home Davy; you don't need them Frenchie girls."

"Might as well," Davy grinned cheekily, "Bit of female company does us all good. You coming with us?"

"No... Think I'll stay here."

Suddenly there was a sound of rapid gunfire, Bill startled, grabbed his gun, cocked his rifle and turned on Davy.

"It's not over Davy," he shouted waving his gun around. "Get down mate, get down"

"Whoa, mate, whoa..." Davy took the gun from him and propped it by the bench. "You don't need that now. It's just the lads letting loose their guns, using up the ammunition. Have a drink Bill, celebrate, the war's done." Davy took a swig from the bottle. There's plenty more where this came from."

He took the bottle and offered it to Bill. "Have a drink ... it'll help... Make you feel better."

"No ta Davy, I don't really drink the stuff,

Davy smiled, "I don't really Bill, I spill most of It." He laughed uproariously, at his joke. Bill laughed with him.

"Go on Bill, have a drink," Davy said again,

"May be I will later," Bill smiled and sat down heavily on the sandbags; his hands were shaking, his heart thumping. The sounds of laughter and singing echoed along the trench.

Davy sat next to Bill and patted arm, "It is over mate," "It really is." Sergeant Monks now rather dishevelled and carrying two bottles of wine returned.

"Where you had them from?" Davy asked

"The Frenchie's come over and give us a crate of the stuff. Lieutenant Thomas said we could take what we wanted." He looked at Bill. "Is he alright?"

Davy shook his head. He held out his and Bill's tin mugs – Sergeant Monks filled them with wine and sits on sandbags opposite Bill and Davy. He handed the mug to Bill. "A toast ... to the end of this god forsaken war. We're going home, leave this all behind us." Davy and Sergeant monks raised their mugs into the air but Bill put his by his side.

Bill looked at the two men. "What we going home to? What's waiting for us?

Davy took a photo from his coat pocket. "I'm going back to my Betty, She's waiting for me."

"And I've got Millie," Sergeant Monks added, "and the kids. Who've you got Bill?"

"Just mother and father, it'll be nice to see them again. I hope Mr Haughton's still got a job for me.

"We were all promised our jobs back at the steel works;" Sergeant Monks said, "it was hard enough getting work before this lot started. Don't know what I'll do if I haven't got a job."

"Yeah, They did say we'd be looked after when we joined up. I hope they'll keep their word."

The three men looked at each other, the celebratory mood was now subsiding. Sergeant Monks them stood up and drained his mug. "Well lads, we're leaving in ten minutes for the village. Anything you want you can buy. But take my advice - Be on your best behaviour - don't touch the women." He patted Davy's shoulder and left the trench leaving the two men alone.

"Whatever we're going back to Bill," Davy said kindly. "We'll sort it out in Blighty. But for now lets enjoy ourselves, lets be thankful that we survived. We can leave here now." He put down the bottle next to Bill, shrugged his shoulders and staggered back down the trench humming a song.

As Davy's singing faded Bill was alone. He looked around him, in the distance the laughter and merriment had increased, the men were celebrating.

"Hear that." He smiled cocking his head, listening, "The guns have stopped, big bertha, silenced for good. That's something to smile about; Fred would have been glad. He couldn't stand the noise." a pained expression crossed his face. "They all would."

There was a long pause then he said, "Should be happy; made it through, just a bit of shrapnel in my leg. That was lucky; some people will say I'm charmed...all I know is that I'm here – alive." He shook his head. "But I don't feel glad, or jubilation, I'm numb, can't think yet, hasn't sunk in." He sat down on the sandbags, picked up his rifle and began to clean it.

"What am I doing?" He threw the rifle on the ground, "Can't shake the habit. Keep it clean. Sergeant Prosser used to tell us, a dirty gun won't look after you." He began to smile, "Well it looked after me." He began to laugh and picked up the rifle, "Yes, you looked after me." He laughed hysterically, "You looked after me oh yes, but you didn't look after Fred, oh no not you, you held the bullet that was going to kill him and I pulled the trigger."

He threw the gun down again and began to cry holding his head in his hands. "Why am I still alive, why didn't one of them bullets get me, there was enough of them." Bill shook his head. "They got Harold and Sergeant Prosser, I was next to them so why didn't one of them bullets have my name on it. I should be dead, shouldn't be here without them. All this guilt weighs heavy...." Bill wiped his eyes. "Stanley Jenkins," he smiled. "Poor fella, not knowing what to do, heard he copped for it, at Ypres. He didn't have to fight, too old, but he did. He joined up that very day. Whatever will become of his family now? He believed their lies. We all believed their bloody lies, and came out here to fight together, to die together. Where was the sense in all this? Fighting, some long forgotten reason... Makes me sick...the poor sods, thousands of them never going home...at least I've lived to tell the tale..." he began to laugh hysterically.

He lifted his head, skywards; a dark cloud was passing over. He smelled the air. "It's going to rain," He said "I can smell it, that lovely fresh smell of rain, that makes everything clean." His foot knocked against the bottle of Brandy left by Davy earlier. He held the bottle up.

"I suppose I should celebrate. Celebrate what, - their deaths. Taken before their time god rest your souls their bodies lying buried somewhere in this mud." He took a swig from the bottle. "Well here's to you lads, a toast to all the dead."

A jagged streak lightening ripped through the sky and thunder crashed overhead. In the flash of light a green mist appeared in the corner of the trench. Bill turned towards it. Standing there before him were the spectres of his friends.

"No," he screamed, "NO…AM I MAD, CAN'T GET RID OF THEM, there they all are, always in the shadows." He pointed to them. "I should be with you; I know that. I feel the guilt; it stabs at my heart like the cold steel of the bayonet. But I'm the one who's going back and face them all. What shall I tell them, lads, when they ask me how you all died? …Tommy fought bravely Mrs Fisher, Harold died peacefully Mrs Braithwaite, You'd have been proud of your only son Mrs Wilkes…Lies, all lies, bloody lies.  We were shivering cowering wrecks, scared of dying, and knowing that death was our fate. Obeying every damnable order, even to shoot our own and why, because if we didn't, it would have been us. Tell me lads will they recognise me, and see that fear in this soldiers eyes."

Bill paused staring at the spectres. He began to laugh manically. "But you won't be staying here, will you lads, not my mates, not staying here. Fred Albert Tommy, Harold Jacko Sgt Prosser, Capt Stubbs, Ernie, Jabez. No, you won't be staying here, not my mates, not staying here."  He laughed hysterically. "You'll make sure this war will never be over, for me, because I've got to remember my brave lads," he laughs again, "because, you'll all be coming home with me." He shouts his fingers tapping hard against his forehead. "We'll never be apart now lads, you'll never leave me now - Because you're all in HERE."

Suddenly Davy ran to Bill. "You alright Bill" he said, "Who you talking to?"

"Davy" Bill looked nervously around him his voice trembling. "No one mate - no one here."
Davy took hold of Bill's arm. "Then come with us and have a real chat to those nice Frenchie ladies, with their ruby red lips and their rosy cheeks. And their warm voluptuous curves." He laughed as he mimicked the ladies hourglass figures with his hands.

Bill moved away from him. "I can't," he yelled, "don't want to leave them. I'm staying here."

Davy looked about him. "Didn't know you were fond of the rats Bill." He sniggered, "That's all that's left here mate." Davy turned to go. Bill shook his head,

"You're right Davy," he laughed nervously, "no-one here." He began to follow Davy along the trench. As he reached the bend he looked back. The spectres were still there, all staring straight at him.

## Sunday 11<sup>th</sup> November 1973

Bill peered intently into the fire, his hands shook; he clasped them tightly together. "After I saw the ghosts of the lads, and Captain Stubbs in that trench, I knew I'd never be free of 'em, they'd be coming home with me but when that was going to be I didn't know. We never got over the loss of Captain Stubbs. He was a gentleman in every sense of the word. He'd been with us throughout, but killing one of his own pushed him over the edge. We never thought he would do anything like that but that's what the war did to folk, made 'um do desperate things. Poor fella, he had a wife and two little children, you know,"

"He must have been at the end of his tether, to have done such a dreadful thing like that." said Beattie

Bill nodded, "He must have been, but he wasn't the only one, there were others…. We were sick of it, mud, rats, lice and death all around. You lost some of your self-respect, living in that filth. You looked at death as an inevitable outcome and some of the lads, rather than waiting for that German bullet used one of their own to end the misery."

Beattie could feel the hot tears filling her eyes. Turning away from Bill, she removed her handkerchief from her apron and dabbed her eyes, then placing her hand on his arm said. "Bill, you don't have to do this. If it's upsetting you…"

Not taking his eyes from the fire, and as if not hearing Beattie, Bill continued to speak. "After the Somme our battalion had been decimated, only a few of us left, and only Albert and Jabez, of the lads that I'd joined up with. Eventually we went to another battalion, another Captain, another sergeant, other soldiers, lads the same as us. We soon settled in, didn't have a choice. But Jabez and Albert were not so lucky; they were both killed a year later, at Passchendaele."

Beattie sighed, "So you had lost them all, all the lads who had joined up, your friends had gone. I don't know how you survived Bill,"

"I suppose you'd say I was lucky, but I didn't think so. As I said, we thought the war was never going end, then 11th November 1918 the news came - the bells rang out - it was over, finally over. We couldn't wait to go back home, back to our families, to our lives, and glad in that respect, but unsure of the future held. Then the orders came; we were to stay in France until further notice to help out over there. We were so angry, at boiling point, ten's of thousands of us refused to stay, demanded we go back to blightly.. We hoped we'd have jobs to go to, after all, they had promised us there would be, but we'd no faith in what the government said, they'd lied from the beginning, how could you trust them again?

Threats of mutiny echoed among the ranks. We had done our bit, lost a lot of good lads, but they still wanted us to give more. We heard some of the French troops had already downed their guns and risked being shot for desertion; they ended up in prison. It was rumoured that thousands of Germans had given themselves up. So we were only following suit. What could they do, we were trained fighting soldiers and we were armed.

Revolution was stirring in the camps, the Russians had got rid of the Tsar and we could do the same with our lot. But that was not a thought we nurtured. The majority of us liked our royal family; after all we had taken the kings shilling.

But the government, they were to be hated, what could they do about those feelings we were contemplating.

Yes Beattie, even I was prepared to go with them, me of all people. But I really wanted to come home, to come back to some normality after the craziness that I'd endured for 4 long years. The whole world had changed, because of that damn war; nothing was ever going to be the same again.

Eventually they began to send us home and in 1919 I boarded the train. But I didn't know what to expect, I knew how I felt and I knew what memories I had brought with me, but how I would deal with them was beyond me. But life went on and I had to live mine. Although I felt dead inside I had to go on living.

# CHAPTER FOURTEEN

1919
And Now the War is Over

The war had been over for four months before Bill had finally got his ticket home. After the Armistice he had been assigned to clearing the trenches and burying the dead. He had done the job void of emotion, just dug the graves and put the bodies in. But then his ticket came, he was to make ready for home.

Bill sat in the railway carriage compartment with eight other soldiers all cramped together. At last they were on their way. He didn't know the men but they were all friendly, happy to be going home, glad to have survived the horrors they had gone through. Bill looked through the window.

In the fields newborn lambs frolicked in the warm spring sunshine. The ripening corn blew in the gentle breeze. Bill saw two horses ploughing in the meadow. His thoughts drew to the horses he had seen in the fields of France, stuck in the mud of Flanders, blown to smithereens by German shells, screaming from the pain of broken limbs and the final insult, butchered for meat for the starving French people. This was the reward for their loyalty. He closed his eyes trying to dismiss the thought.

"Like a smoke mate?" a young soldier sitting opposite him offered a packet of French cigarettes to him.

Bill smiled; his shaking hand reached for the packet. The soldier smiled, and taking a cigarette, handed it to him.

"Thanks," said Bill. He lit it, took a long drag and coughed deeply. "Never got used to these," he said.

He looked out of the window. The train whistle blew; they were in a tunnel, darkness engulfed the carriage. The lights dimly flickered. Bill gazed at his reflection in the window. How he had changed, aged beyond his years. What would they think of him back home?

Suddenly a figure appeared behind him, may be one of the lads had stood up, he turned to check, no one had moved. He turned back to the window; the figure, still there reflected in the glass. Bill's eyes narrowed, he focused on the image. The figure slowly turned towards him; "Oh God its Albert." His hands clasped his face.

Now the other soldiers in the carriage were staring, watching him. He looked from one to the other, to his horror; their faces were changing, changing into the faces of his friends, Tommy Albert, Jacko Jabez Harold, Ernie, Captain Stubbs, Sgt Prosser....Fred.

"No, No!" he yelled, "Leave me, go away."

"You alright mate?" the young man sitting opposite touched his arm. Bill jerked his head up. The train had passed through the tunnel; sunlight streamed into the carriage dispelling the last traces of the darkness. The other soldiers were staring at him with sympathetic glances and knowing smiles.

"Yes mate," Bill sighed, "I'm alright now." He looked out of the window again. The warmth from the sun's rays enveloped him; reluctantly his eyes began to close. Soon sleep would follow, and within that sleep, were the spectres of his friends waiting in the darkness.

As the white cloudy steam escaping from the engine's chimney began to clear Bill could see in the distance the railway station, adorned with brightly coloured streamers, and buntings billowing in the gentle breeze, a brass band played it's a long way to Tipperary to the beat of the big bass drum.

He sighed heavily and leaned back in the seat. They would be there, his family, friends, and Emma. What would he tell her about Albert, what would he tell all of them, the truth? No; he shook his head...never....

If only he could get off the train before it pulled into the station, make his way across the fields to home. But the train was slowing down, screeching and jolting as the brakes were applied, the whistle announcing its arrival, finally coming to rest by the dangerously crowded platform.

The carriage doors swung open, Bill lined up in the corridor with the rest of the men and joined the shuffling line waiting to exit the train. He looked out of the window, the noisy throng, cheering, shouting, and waving flags and the band played with such gaiety. He saw the young soldiers swallowed up within the swelling crowd and enveloped in the arms of their loved ones. Then he caught sight of his sister Elsie, jostling through the crowds towards the carriages. He leaned out of an open window.

"Elsie," he shouted, "Elsie."

"Bill," she smiled waving vigorously, He waved back.

"Come on mate, Get a move on." the soldier behind nudged him,

"Sorry, sorry." Bill apologised and moved along the line. Finally he reached the doorway and stepped onto the platform, the rapturous applause and backslapping had not lessened as he made his way through the crowd.

"Bill, over here" Elsie called. Her warm smile filled his heart with joy. He edged his way towards her.

"It's good to see you Elsie," he said,
She wrapped her arms around him. "And you Bill. You're home now, that's all that matters."

Bill opened the front door of his childhood home and stepped inside. The aroma of freshly baked bread was wafting from the kitchen. His mother, busy at the stove had not yet heard him. For a few seconds he stood and watched her, a lump in his throat, his heart brimming with love. "Hello Ma."

Mrs Gibson gave a gasp and her wooden spoon clattered to the floor. She turned and ran to her son, wrapping her arms around him. "Oh Bill, how I've prayed for this day, oh son, oh my boy!" She pressed him tight against her, tears rolling down her plump cheeks.

"There, there Ma, its good to see you too," said Bill. "How have you been?"
Mrs Gibson held her son at arms length now and stroked his face tenderly. "Oh never mind me, let me have a look at you, oh let me look at you!" she cried lifting the hem of her apron to wipe her tears. "Oh you've grown so thin son!"

"No! Its just this uniform," laughed Bill.

"We must feed you up, now, sit down, kettle's just boiled. We're having your favourite for tea, potato hash with a crust on. But I'll get you some bread and cheese for now, it's from Mr Haughton's farm…"

"Don't fuss Mum -"

"Of course I must fuss, now sit yourself down."

"I've been sitting down for three hours on the train-"

"Never mind, you must rest. Now Elsie get a plate"

Mrs Gibson bustled about the kitchen, cutting several thick slices of her homemade crusty bread and piling it on to the large oval plate Elsie had provided with a generous chunk of cheddar and pickles, all the while providing her son with an animated account of all that had happened in the village during his absence.

"Mr Haughton says he'll be more than glad to have you back on the farm whenever you're ready…" Said Elsie "told me to tell you, when he knew you were coming back…he said go up…go and see him …when you're ready…"

"There's time enough for that, in a bit, Elsie." Mrs Gibson quickly interrupted, "he's only just home poor lad, don't be sending him off again."

"Haughton's farm's not the Western Front ma!" laughed Elsie.

"I know, I know, and I thank God for that," said Mrs Gibson. "Oh Bill I can't tell you what it feels like to have you home, oh I'm going to cry again, sorry I just can't help it."

"I know Mum," said Elsie gently squeezing her mother's hand, "but our Bill doesn't want to see you so upset."

"I'm not upset, I'm happy, happy my boy's home for good." She set off in a fresh flood of tears and she hugged and kissed them both.

When Mrs Gibson had dried her eyes again she poured the tea and sat down with Bill and Elsie at the kitchen table.

"Now listen, your father will be back soon and he's bringing Aunt Bertha, you know she thinks a lot of you Bill, I hope you don't mind, - oh talk of the devil, here they are now."

The front door had opened and Mr Gibson's voice could be heard, "Come in Bertha, make yourself at home – hey up, I believe we've got another visitor."

"Hardly a visitor!" exclaimed Bertha as her eyes lighted on her nephew. "Bill, oh love, give your Auntie Bertha a hug!"

Bill rose to his feet and embraced his aunt.

"Oh you're as handsome as ever," said Bertha.

"Takes after his father," said Mr Gibson, grasping his son's hand fit to crush it. "Welcome home son."

"He does look thin though," said Bertha.

"That's what I said," agreed Mrs Gibson.

"Oh we'll soon fatten him up," said her husband, slapping Bill's shoulder heartily.

Elsie laughed, "You make him sound like a Christmas turkey Dad!"

"Bill, now there's a few people as want to see you," said Mrs Gibson, "and I thought that we could have a little welcome home party, what do you think?"

"Well I -"

Before Bill could answer, his Aunt Bertha interrupted, "Your mother wasn't sure exactly when you would get back Bill, but I thought I would bring this for you." Delving in her handbag she took out a small brown paper parcel and handed it to her nephew.

"What is it?" asked Bill.

"Open it and find out lad," said Bertha.

Bill carefully untied the string and removed the paper to reveal a small shiny object.

"It's the lucky silver cat," beamed Bertha proudly. "All the while you were gone," she said, her voice trembling now, "I spoke to it, every day, asking it to look after you. And it did. It's yours now."

Bill gazed at the pendant, turning it over in his palm.

Mrs Gibson broke the silence, "Potato hash won't be long everyone, let's go and sit in the parlour for a bit. Bill why don't you get changed out of that uniform, there's clean clothes in your drawer."

"Yes, you get freshened up lad," said Mr Gibson. "But I want you back in that uniform and looking smart when we go down the pub tonight. I want to show you off. George Finney's lad's back, been home for a while now. George brings him down in his wheelchair and Mr Barnett set him a special place at the end of the bar. George will glad to see you."

Bill looked uneasy. "He's lost both legs Dad, and his right eye's gone. Why would he want to see me, to talk about what a good time we all had out there?"

"I know what you're saying lad," said Mr Gibson, placing a fatherly hand on Bill's arm, "but it might do you both good – two heroes returned!"

"NO!" The room fell silent. Bill's face was quivering with distress. "I'm sorry," he said, "I didn't mean to shout, just not tonight please Dad. Mum was right, I think I am a bit tired…the train journey and all."

Mr Gibson patted his son's shoulder, "All right Bill, whatever you want."

"Thanks Dad," he said, "I'll go and change now, I'll be down in a while."

Bill looked around his bedroom, the warm, safe place he had known since he was a little boy. The old familiar things he had left behind a century ago it seemed, were still in their place – the makeshift boat his Dad had carved out of a log of wood one Christmas, his favourite books, even the well worn teddy bear – all lovingly dusted and watched over by his mother as she had counted the days, filled with anxiety, of her son's absence.

He took off his uniform and dropped it in a heap on the floor. Putting on a clean shirt and trousers he stared at his reflection in the wardrobe mirror. How he had changed in four years, the horrors he had seen etched into his young face, the things he had done recorded on his scarred hands; he had managed to stop them trembling when he was downstairs, but he noticed the shaking was coming back again. Right now he had something to do, something he must do.
Turning from the mirror he gathered the uniform in his arms and walked back downstairs.

Grateful to find the kitchen now empty, Bill slipped out of the back door into the garden. The old rusty bathtub was still at the far end where it had always been, just far enough from the house and the sheds. He threw the uniform onto the old ashes, arranged some bits of wood around the clothes then struck a match and lit the paper. The fire quickly took, the corners of the khaki fabric already beginning to singe and blacken. As the flames licked higher Bill felt something leaving him, some great inner cry of release, resignation and despair.

He stared at the smouldering remains. All that was left of his uniform was a pile of ashes. Now he felt only numb, dead inside. It seemed to him that this was what his life was now. There was to be no more real laughter, no more actual joy, but instead he would go through the motions, play acting like one of the strolling players they had seen in the taverns in France, or the cheap comical shows his dad had once taken him to watch at the seaside.

He would be the poor player, strutting and fretting his hours on stage, working, laughing, loving even, but it would all be a sham. Inside he was as dead as his comrades who were even now being eaten by worms in Flanders. The only difference was he had been the one to come home.

After an evening of his mother's constant fussing, his father's forced joviality and Aunt Bertha's tearful smiles, Bill could take no more and retired to bed early. As he closed the bedroom door he could hear them whispering in concerned tones about him. Too weary to care or to close the curtains, he sat down heavily on the bed.

The moon was almost full, and the trees on the distant hills were silhouetted against the night sky. Soon he would sleep and then would come the unremitting dreams. He clasped his trembling hands together as the memory of Ernie came to him again. Tomorrow he would see Nancy and keep his promise.

Reaching for his kit bag he took out a bottle of whisky and took a long swig. The alcohol seared his throat but he was used to that now. "Let's see if you can sweeten my dreams tonight," he said aloud, "Oh God please yes, most of all tonight."

---

# CHAPTER FIFTEEN

A Promise to Keep

Bill stood on the pavement outside the small terraced house. He took a deep breath, straightened his cap and knocked three times on the shiny green paint of the front door. She's not in he thought, and with a feeling of relief turned to depart.

Just then the door opened. A homely smell of beeswax polish and baking wafted out. "Hello Bill," said Nancy, "I heard you were back, won't you come in?"

Nancy's kind smile touched his heart. He took off his cap. "Thanks."

"Would you like a cup of tea?"

"No – yes, all right, thanks."

Nancy laughed, "You're out of the army now Bill, no need to stand on ceremony. Expect you're glad to be out of uniform too aren't you? So long as there's a job in Civvy Street I suppose."

"Mr. Haughton's offered to have me back," said Bill.

"So they should, good workers like you don't come ten a penny."

Bill followed Nancy through to the kitchen where a fire was burning brightly in the grate. "I was just catching up on a bit of housework."

"Oh I'm sorry.."

"No, no, glad to take a break."

A clean white cloth covered the table, and a jam jar filled with roses stood in the centre. Next to the sugar bowl was a jug of milk covered with a small, embroidered cloth with small coloured beads sewn round the edge to weight it down.

"Sit down Bill. I've just made these scones, would you like one with some jam on? I've only got damson at the moment, not got round to making any other flavours yet."

"Yes, thank you, that will be lovely." Bill pulled out a chair and sat rather stiffly. On the polished sideboard, he noticed in pride of place a photograph of Ernie and Nancy on their wedding day. Their joyful, innocent expressions said it all, a young couple very much in love.

Nancy set the table with two china cups, saucers and plates and put the plate of scones next to them. She poured the steaming tea and handed a cup to Bill. Seeing Bill looking at the wedding picture she said, "I do miss him you know."

"I'm sure you do, he was a good man."

She smiled, "He had his moments mind."

"Who doesn't?"

"That's true, but he was the only man for me Bill, I don't want anyone else, and I never will."

"You will be alright though Nancy?"

She smiled kindly, "I've got this house; it's not much but its mine, me job in the tripe shop and a bundle of wonderful memories. He'll be in my heart forever. I'll be all right Bill…Now, help yourself to sugar and a scone, don't be shy."

Bill bit into the pastry. "These are good Nancy, you're a fine cook."

"Kind of you to say so, but you've not come here to tell me how good my scones are."

Bill lowered his gaze, "No, I've not."

"So what have you come for?"

"I made Ernie a promise Nancy, that if I got out alive I would come and see you when I got back."

"Oh, well, here you are."

"There's more. Ernie was proud of you, never stopped talking about you – Nancy this, Nancy that - told me to tell you that he loved you very much."

"Oh the daft apeth', I know he did, he told me in his last letter. Nancy's face then grew sombre. "Bill, can I ask, what was it like for you out there, for the two of you? How was it for Ernie, at the end? I feel it might somehow be a comfort, to know everything - if you know what I mean."

Bill breathed heavily. He saw the walls of the trench closing around him, the squelching mud below. "I can't Nancy, I don't want to remember."

Nancy placed her hand on his, "I'm sorry, you've been through enough, I spoke out of turn."

Bill's eyes filled with tears. "That's what Ernie did, put his hand on mine and gripped it so tight. *'Promise me, he said, promise me you'll tell her how much I love her.'* He was so scared, we all were…we knew what was coming…I'm sorry Nancy, you've no idea, what we saw, it was awful…" Bill's tears were falling now.

----

"It's alright Bill, I understand -"

"No you don't! I'm sorry, I'm sorry, its just that, no one does, no one can.... no one ever will..."

Bill closed his eyes, sending more tears dropping onto the white tablecloth. "Sorry, not very manly to cry is it. Chin up, that's what we're all told."

"You cry as much as you want Bill, I'm not judging. I'm not the one that's done what you've done."

"And Ernie, oh Ernie was right there in the thick of it. It was the night before the Somme, just before we were to go over the top. All the battalions were marching to the front line, we were just settling in, when Ernie came with his lot. He was his usual blustering self..."

Nancy gave a wistful smile. "And I bet he was having a right old go at me. Oh I know what he was like Bill, so don't try to spare my feelings."

"Well no, it wasn't like that. He told us he'd got married to you..."

"And made an honest woman of me at last. I bet that's what you all thought, and had a good laugh at my expense."

"No Nancy, nothing likes that. We just couldn't believe that Ernie Fowles was wed, that was all. He stayed with us for a while, the same old Ernie, bragging and boasting, but I saw something was different about him. He told us how he'd been burying some of the lads that had come a cropper a few days earlier. It was obviously playing on his mind, but there was something else. It was you Nancy. He missed you and he wanted to be home. He wished he'd listened to you. We sat together and that's when he grabbed my hand, I've never known a man grip so tight, not even my dad. *'If I don't make it Bill, he said, if I don't get through all this ...promise me you'll tell her how much I wanted to come home to her, how much I miss her. Tell her I love her - love her with all my heart. Promise me Bill - promise you'll do that for me.'* I told him not to be so daft and that we'd both be home soon, but I made the promise anyway. The next second there was this almighty bang and a shell had exploded right over our heads. We all dived for cover and then Ernie got up, dusted himself off and walked away, back to his battalion. That was the last time I saw him. The next day we went over the top."

Bill's hand had begun to shake, and fresh tears were welling in his eyes. "It was hell out there, none of us knew if we'd survive the next few minutes never mind make it home. I thought I'd never keep the promise to Ernie, but I'm here and I don't know how." Bill clenched his teeth hard as if hit by a sudden excruciating pain, "I feel so bad about that."

Nancy held Bill's hand tightly. "Come on now Bill it's done with, finished. Ernie was unlucky, you came home; there's no rhyme or reason to it."

"That's the point," groaned Bill. Still in agony he buried his head in his hands. "That's what makes it so terrible. Life and death, if there is a God how does he decide who lives or dies?"

Nancy stroked his head tenderly, "Ernie would be eternally grateful to know you've come here today. Come on now Bill, its done with, finished,"

"It's not, Nancy," he sobbed, "not for me."

## Sunday 11ᵗʰ November 1973

And that's about it. The rest as they say is history."
Beattie's hand remained on Bill's. "I never knew what you'd gone through Bill," she said quietly, "never realised…"
Bill sighed. "No one did Beattie. It might sound selfish or that we're claiming to be something special, but that's the whole point, we weren't special, we were ordinary men. No one who hadn't been there could ever understand what it was like. God willing no one will have to do so ever again."
"And what of Nancy Bill?"
Bill gave wry thoughtful smile. "She never married again. *'He's the love of my life'* she used to tell me."
"So you kept in touch with her,"
"For a while, just to see if she was alright you know. But Nancy would manage; she had done all her life." He chuckled, "Its funny you know, marrying Ernie has given her some sort of respectability. There were a few fella's chasing her but she didn't give them the time of day. No, Ernie was the only one for her. You see Beattie, that damn war didn't care who it destroyed."
There was a knock at the front door. Bill looked at the clock. "It's only one o'clock, Paul's not coming till three he said."
"Now don't start worrying," said Beattie, "I'll let him in." She walked to the hallway and opened the door. Bill listened intently.
"What can I do for you?" asked Beattie. There came a muffled reply then Beattie called out, "Bill, there's someone to see you, says his name's Walter."
"I don't know anyone by that name," replied Bill, "best show him in."
Beattie reappeared, followed by a man of similar age to Bill. "Please forgive the uninvited visit Mr Gibson," he said.
"Have we met?" said Bill looking mystified.
"No, you don't know me, but you knew my brother. I've been trying to find out more about him and I was wondering if I could ask for your help."
"I will if I can, but I'm not sure I ever knew your brother. Look, have a seat, anywhere." Walter chose a seat at the table and Bill sat down next to him. Beattie stood and watched in silence. Bill stared at the visitor. "Are you sure its me you want?"

"Oh yes Mr Gibson, its definitely you."

Walter pulled a faded sepia photograph from his inside coat pocket and handed it to Bill. "This is my brother, taken on his first home leave."

Bill put on his glasses and squinted at the picture. He shook his head, "No I can't say I recognise -" He broke off and looked at Walter then at the photograph again. "Oh my Lord," he said in a hushed voice, "Fred - its Fred Carter."

As he held the picture closer to the light Beattie noticed his hand begin to shake. She placed her hand on his shoulder, "Bill, what is it love?"

"I'm sorry, would you leave me now, please," said Bill querulously. "Go, please."

Beattie motioned to Walter to get up. As he did so Bill gripped his arm. "Not you, I want to talk to you."

"I'll leave you two alone then," said Beattie gently. "Sure you're all right Bill?"

"I will be, I'm sorry Beattie I just need -"

"It's alright Bill, I understand. I'll look in later."


When she had gone Walter said, "I'm very sorry Mr Gibson, I didn't mean to cause you any distress."

"You've not. At least- " Bill took a handkerchief from his pocket and wiped his eyes. "Just a bit of a shock that's all, seeing him again after all this time."

"I'm sure. I should have phoned or written first, not just turned up out of the blue. I'm sorry."

"Don't be," said Bill. "Would have given me a jolt either way." He handed the photo back to Walter. "Well, so you must be his brother."

"You're right, I'm him."

"I remember him saying to me he hoped he didn't get into trouble…"

Walter smiled, "He was always looking after me was our Fred."

"So now you've met one of your brothers old comrades, what do you want to ask me?"

"You knew Fred, Mr Gibson, the two of you fought side by side and went through hell together. I want to know what he was like over there. I want to know what happened to him, I want to hear the truth Mr Gibson. You see when my mother died last year, me and my wife were sorting through her belongings when we came across this letter."

Walter produced a small, yellowing envelope from which he pulled out a crinkled letter. "I had never seen this before, Mother never showed it to me. She always said Fred died a hero, died in battle, and I believed her. My father never came back from the war, bought it in Gallipoli. I don't know if he even knew about Fred. Why did it end like that for him? Would you like to see what Fred wrote?" Bill's face was expressionless, his eyes staring hard at Walter. "All right," he said. Putting his glasses back on he cleared his throat and read aloud:

*My dearest Mother, Father and Walter*

*I hope by now you will have had the news. I am sorry for the trouble I have caused you and father. I tried to be strong and to keep my wits about me, but it was all too much. In your eyes I have disgraced our good name and for this I am paying the price. I hope in time you all will forgive me and understand my reasoning.*

*I'm not a coward, not like they say but if that's what is deemed to be, then who am I to tell it differently. Bill Gibson is a good mate, he looked after me that very first time we went over the top.*

*Reverend Pennymore is with me so I'm not alone and I thank god for that. He's very kind and is helping me to write this letter. We've said a prayer and I feel better now, quite calm in fact, like a heavy weight has been lifted.*

*But this time will pass and one day there will be peace, a time when no more innocent blood will be spilt, maybe then you will think kindly of me.*

*The sun is coming up now, its nearly time. I'm not scared, but sad for all of you, and sad that we will never see each other again in this life. I am sorry for bringing dishonour upon you all. Try to forget my faults and remember me only as your very loving son.*

*Please forgive me.*

*Fred.*

Bill replaced the letter in the envelope and handed it back to Walter. "What do I tell them when they seek me out?" he said.

"What was that Mr Gibson?"

A forlorn smile flickered for a second on Bill's face.

"Nothing Walter, nothing," he replied. "Tell me, how did you find me?"

"I took the letter to Fred's old battalion. They were very dismissive, told me very little. I asked them if they knew you, they told me you'd survived the war and gave me this address. My wife didn't want me to come here, thought I should forget about Fred. But I had to. I couldn't rest without speaking to one of Fred's old comrades. I apologise Mr Gibson, I'm sure I'm stirring up the past in a way you might not welcome, having been out there yourself."

Bill drew in a long breath. The memories were surfacing that was for sure, and they were frighteningly clear. Now there was poor Fred's brother to reckon with.

"That's all right," said Bill patting the other man's arm, "you've nothing to reproach yourself for. I can imagine how it must have felt to discover that letter. I'll tell you what I remember about your brother. I first met him in a little café the night before we were going up to the front line. He was a very polite fellow, very amiable, and we had a drink or two together with some of the other lads. Later on when we were in the trench he turned up, a new recruit to our battalion. The look on his face said it all. The rest of us were used to the conditions by then, not that we found them pleasant by a long chalk, but I suppose we were resigned to that side of it. Fred didn't really know what else was coming."

"The Germans you mean?" said Walter.

"He was still buying the old patriotic lie, the propaganda, and who could blame him? He also thought it was going to be easy in some way. We were all gullible in the beginning, that's why we joined up, and for what – what were we?"

"Cannon fodder?"

"You said it son."

"So what happened then, did Fred go into battle with the rest of you?"

145

Bill nodded, "Oh yes, your brother was with us. We'd been waiting some while in that trench, all of us tired, nervous, scared, we knew what was waiting for us. The shelling was terrible and you never knew when one was going to land on you, that or a sniper's bullet. I think we'd all seen men dying by our sides one way or another. But Fred hadn't. An hour before we went over the top, listening to some of the other blokes, the penny dropped with him. Then when he heard the machine guns open up and some fella screaming, that did it, he was like a bag of jelly. We were all scared, each and every one of us, but Fred was terrified, could hardly stand up. I grabbed him, told him to stay with me. Then before we knew it the whistles all along the line blew."

"That was your signal?"

"Up the ladders and out into no man's land. Fred went up and I followed him. We stayed close. Men were falling all around us - never seen so many drop at once, our mates - good lads – dead…screaming, shouting, the noise of the guns. Sergeant Prosser, Harold killed at our side, bullets whizzing past our heads, shells falling everywhere, it was chaos, bloody chaos."

"But you kept going forward."

"There was no other choice, it was either that or be shot by our own side for cowardice then a shell exploded right by us. I fell to my knees, coughing, choking in the smoke, my leg feeling like it was on fire. I looked for Fred but he was nowhere. Next thing I knew the stretcher lads had taken me and I woke up in the field hospital."

"You must have thought Fred was already a goner."

"I couldn't see him among the wounded, so yes I thought he'd been killed out there, that day. It was only when I got back to my unit I found out he'd been court marshalled for cowardice, running away from the enemy."

Walter's face was ashen. "So its true what the battalion told me, Fred was a coward, that's why they shot him."

Bill stood up and walked to the window. The autumn leaves were falling gently in the back garden. "Fred was no coward," he said quietly. "Just a lad scared to death. When the shell knocked us all to the ground Fred got up and carried on walking towards what he thought were the enemy gun emplacements. But in the smoke he was confused."

"You mean to say -"

Bill turned back to face Walter. "He couldn't see a thing. He was walking the wrong way, back towards our trenches. He told his superiors but they wouldn't listen."

Walter had an intense expression on his face, "But I mean, how can we know he was telling the truth?"

"I spoke to several of the men who saw Fred firing as he walked, shouting defiance at the Germans. So unless he was trying to kill his own blokes..." Bill tailed off.

"But he was shot at dawn, shot by his own battalion." Walter's tone was bitter now.

Bill bowed his head. "Yes Walter he was. I remember the day very clearly. As I woke up I saw the sun rising, beautiful and golden, breaking through the darkness of the night. For a moment I thought I was back on the farm with the horses."

"Did you see Fred before they shot him."

Bill nodded, "I had to."

Walter, with a strain in his voice said slowly, "What do you mean you had to?"

Bill turned back to the window. "Well you see Walter, I was one of them that did it."

Walter stared. "What?"

"I was one of the firing squad. I was ordered to, not that that excuses anything."

Walter hung his head. "Oh my god."

"He was brave when they brought him out," Bill said quietly. "Even gave us a smile. Not a mad smile you understand but...oh, I don't know how to describe it, it was like, a sign of peace. When they tied him to the post he panicked for a second but then he was calm again. When the order was given to aim he lifted his head, as if he were looking towards heaven."

Walter's voice was also trembling now. "Was it...was it quick."

Bill hesitated. "The captain had to finish him off, took out his revolver and put a bullet in his head. That did it."

Walter was clenching and unclenching his fists, his jaw working up and down. His shoulders gave a sudden heave and he began crying. "He died for nothing, for a mistake, oh dear god, Fred...!"

"I'm sorry," said Bill. He came over and placed his hand on Walter's arm. "I've lived with the guilt all these years and I'll die with it. All my mates died out there, I should have gone with them." Bill was also crying now.

"What could you have done?" said Walter, "You mustn't blame yourself. But I'm glad you've told me, it makes a difference and I thank you for it. Look, come and sit down, I'd like to tell you about our Fred, may I?"

"All right," said Bill and sat back at the table.

Walter wiped his eyes and composed himself. "My big brother Fred was full of fun, liked a laugh and was always bordering on trouble, but I loved him, he was my best friend."

"Blood's thicker than water," said Bill.

"You're right there Mr Gibson."

"Call me Bill."

"All right Bill, thank you. Well, many a time when we were lads, Fred fought my battles and won, so when the war came along he couldn't wait to join up. Dad had already enlisted and no matter what Mother said, Fred was going to go as well, nothing was going to stop him. When he got his uniform on he wasn't afraid of showing himself off to anyone who admired him, and there were plenty that did." Walter smiled fondly as he pictured his brother in 1914. "He marched off that morning as proud as a peacock, waving as he turned the corner, a young man with his life ahead of him, fighting for king and country. But on his first leave home we saw a difference; he'd changed, grown up, not our Fred anymore; the war had got hold of him. The night before he was going back, I heard him crying, whimpering in his sleep. The next morning he said good-bye, hugged mother, and me so tightly, something he'd never done before. He seemed to know he wasn't coming back. Mother felt it I'm sure. After we got the telegram that he had died, my mother cried every day. I always believed what she told me, but now I know the truth."

Bill said gently, "But there's no shame in that truth Walter. I'm sorry, I shouldn't have told you please forgive me."

"Mr Gibson, you've done nothing to be forgiven for. Fred is still a hero to me, no matter what happened. You didn't kill him, or your friends, the war did that, you were but a small part of it. You would have saved them all if you could have, but you couldn't."

"Your brother did his bit. You should be proud of him."

---

"I am," said Walter. "I can let Fred rest in peace now. And I want you to know you did no wrong, Fred would have known that too. In such a time of madness it could just as easily have been Fred staring down the barrel of a gun at one of his mates."

Bill nodded, "And I'll be the first to admit I could have been a genuine coward, running for cover on purpose."

"It would have been the sane thing to do! And now, if you don't mind me saying so, is the time to leave the past where it is. Your mates suffered for a short time, you've suffered all you life; our Fred wouldn't have wanted that and he wouldn't want you to blame yourself in any way for what happened."

"Thank you Walter."

"You've taken a burden off my shoulders, and I only hopes that our meeting and talking like this has made you feel a little easier in your mind too."

Bill stood up and the two men shook hands. "It has Walter, it has. If you want to look in again any time you know where to find me. I'm expecting to be staying with my son and his family for a while, but Beattie at number forty-six across the road will give you the address if you want to contact me."

"I'll take you up on that Bill, thank you."

When Walter had gone Bill returned to the window and looked out again. The light was fading now. He gazed up at the sky where the old moon was waning and said aloud,

"Did I tell him right Fred? You were brave, all of you were. It's been a long time lads but I think Walter's right. I've got a new life waiting for me with my son. I've been given a second chance and I shouldn't turn it down. I can't take you with me lads, not this time. But I can take the memories, the good ones, and I'll treasure them."

Bill's reverie was interrupted by another knock on the front door. He glanced at the clock on the mantelpiece; five minutes past three.

Taking his stick he shuffled down the hall. "Coming Paul," he called out. He reached the door, his hand trembling as he turned the latch. "It's been a long time Paul -" Bill stopped in mid sentence.

Standing before him was not his son, but the group of teenage boys who only that morning had mocked and tormented him.

149

"I don't want any trouble lads," said Bill attempting to quickly close the door. Before he could do so however a hand had pressed against it from the other side. As he raised his stick in defence it was immediately held by one of the youths. Bill lifted his other arm to shield himself. Then to his surprise, the young man handed his stick back.

"Sorry Mr Gibson," said the youth, "didn't mean to...the thing is...we just wanted to..." As he tailed off inarticulately, one of his companions stepped forward, "What Jason's trying to say, is that we're sorry about this morning."

"Yeah, and the other times," said Jason.

"We were out of order," said a third lad pushing his way to the front. We never understood about you, why you were the way you were, like."

"We just thought you were a grumpy old git," said Jason.

"Don't say that," hissed his friend, giving him a sharp dig in the ribs.

Bill looked at them, five young men full of high spirits, full of promise, looking for a purpose or just something to do with their lives. Confused, vulnerable, too often put upon by meaningless authority, deep down in their hearts, given the chance, they were good, caring young people.

"I'll let you into a secret lads," said Bill.

"What's that?"

"Sometimes I am a grumpy old git!" This provoked a roar of laughter. "And if I've behaved that way to you on certain occasions, then I apologise for it"

"That's all right," the boys chorused. Jason then nudged the leader of the group, who took out a packet of tobacco. "We got you this Mr Gibson," he said handing the packet to Bill. "Smoking isn't good for you but Eddie told us what you like."

Bill took the tobacco. "No, it's not good for you. But at my time of life I think, why not have a little of what you enjoy."

"You deserve to Mr Gibson," said another youth. "What you did, we'd never be able to do that. We're not brave enough to fight like you did."

"Yeah, you're a hero," said Jason. The others murmured in agreement.

"I hope you never have to lads," said Bill, "and thank you."

"No, Mr Gibson, thank you for what you did," said the first youth, "we won't bother you any more. And if there's anything you want doing, let us know. We'll be looking out for you from now on."

Bill, too overcome to say more, nodded and watched the young men walk slowly off. Looking across the road he saw Eddie, who had been observing the scene. Eddie nodded to him. Bill raised his hand in acknowledgement and walked slowly back to the living room.

"Well what a funny old day it's been," Bill said to himself. He placed the packet of tobacco on the table and gazed at it, his mind trying to piece together the events of the last few hours. He wondered who had told the boys about his wartime exploits. Eddie probably. Well, he was grateful to him. He would never have had the nerve to start that sort of conversation himself with the younger generation. He would have been too afraid of laughter or derision.

"You okay Dad? The door was unlocked."

Bill turned to see his son Paul. "Oh, Paul!" In a rush of emotion Bill took his son in his arms.

"That's quite a welcome Dad."

"Its something I've wanted to do for a long time," said Bill. "How many years is it?"

"I've lost count," said Paul. "You and me have got a lot of catching up to do. Are you sure you're all right to travel?"

"Fine, fine, just had a bit of a day of it that's all."

Paul picked up Bill's suitcase from the side of the chair. "Are you ready then?"

Bill looked nonplussed, "Not got time for a brew?"

"Best get ahead of the traffic," said Paul looking at his watch. "We'll stop for a cuppa on route." He put an affectionate hand on his father's shoulder, "in fact there's going to be a hell of a lot of tea drunk between you and me from now on eh?"

Bill suddenly burst into a much-loved old army song: "There was tea, tea, as much as the Irish Sea, in the quartermaster's stores..."

Paul joined his father in the rousing chorus, "My eyes are dim I cannot see, I have not brought my specs with me...!"

"Oh that reminds me," said Bill, "I'll need my spare pair of glasses."

"This them?" said Paul.

---

"Thanks son."

"Back door locked, gas turned off?"

"All done," Bill assured him. He then said, "I know you want to get on the road son, but there's somewhere I would like to look in on before we go."

"Oh, where's that?"

"A place I should have visited a long time ago. It would mean a lot to me if you could take me there now. I'll explain later."

Baffled, Paul looked at his father for a moment. Noting the meaningful look in his eyes he said, "All right Dad, it might be better to wait till the rush hour's over anyway. Lead on."

"No, you go and start the car, I'll be with you in a minute."

"Okay." Paul took the suitcase and went out of the front door.

Bill stood in the hallway. From a hook on the wall hung a heavy black overcoat. He took the coat down and laid his hand on the medals that Mabel had once upon a time pinned to the breast pocket for him. She had tried to persuade him to wear them, but he had kept them here, turned to the wall and out of sight all these years. He tried on the coat; it still fitted him.

Drawing himself up to his full height and adjusting his medals he said, "Right, I think I'm ready now."

## Sunday 11th November 1973

Bill peered out through the windscreen at the thick fog. On such a murky November evening it was hard to see exactly where you were. The headlights of an oncoming vehicle briefly illuminated the signpost to the park.

"Drop me off here Paul, I'll find it easier on foot and I don't want to keep you hanging around.

Paul pulled up beside the pavement and unfastened his seat belt.

"It's all right I'll come in with you Dad. In this weather it's bound to be a bit slippery under foot."

"That's all right I'll take it slow."

"Don't be daft, you can't see your hand in front of your face out there."

"I'll manage, I'll have to."

"Look its no trouble," Paul insisted, "what else am I going to do? I'm coming with you."

Bill shook his head and said firmly, "I told you son, this is one thing I've got to do on my own." He opened the car door, the warmth from the heater clashing with a sudden blast of cold air making him shiver.

Paul sighed, "At least put your cap on then Dad, they say you lose a third of your body heat through your head – here – and take this torch." He passed his father his thick tweed cap and the torch.

Steadying himself on the pavement Bill wrapped his overcoat tightly around him and put on his cap.

"You're sure you're going to be alright?" said Paul. "When do you want me to pick you up?"

"What?" Bill stared into the fog, his mind preoccupied.

"I mean, how long will it take?"

"If only I knew son, but I've never known, never."

"Look I'll go to the car park and wait for you there, if you're not back in 10 minutes I'll come for you.

"I told you Paul, I don't know how long I'll be. Just wait for me."

"Then be careful, mind you don't slip Dad."

"Yes, yes alright, now go," said Bill waving his son on.

Placing one hand on the park railings every few steps, he made his way slowly along the pavement towards the entrance. Reaching the large ornate pillars he lifted the torch. The iron gates were shut. What if they were locked? He hadn't thought of that. It would be a good excuse to walk away. But was that what he wanted? The agony would only go on, the ghosts never be laid.

In the blur of his drinking he been able to ignore them, send them to sleep just as he had slept through days and nights in the oblivion of the bottle. But as surely as daybreak came, the ghosts had always woken again, come to life to dance their tormenting dance of madness, sorrow, and accusation though his fevered thoughts.

"But what if they turn me away now," he thought. What if this mission, this pilgrimage, whatever it was he was trying to do here, turned into another failure?

With a sudden panic Bill felt the urge to turn back, to go home again, to have a drink, anything but –

"Let the gates be locked," he muttered under his breath "oh let 'em be locked!"

This was not a trench in France, he told himself, he was not going 'over the top', and there were no machine guns waiting. So turn around and go. Yet what had to be done now would still take every ounce of his courage.

Bill walked forward a few yards and pushed one of the gates. It swung open noiselessly; the council had always taken good care of the place. The rising moon shone a pallid light through the fog to reveal the path. The War Memorial bathed in its own sombre illumination stood just ahead casting long, eerie shadows over the shrubbery. His hands trembled; that same sickening depth of apprehension filled his thoughts, just as it had all those years ago before he faced those hungry German guns.

For a moment he stopped, the swirling fog was closing in, wrapping him in the dulled silence. Behind, was darkness, the place he had come from, where his son, was waiting to take him to a new life.

Suddenly the gentle hint of wood smoke drifted towards him. The aroma provoked a vivid memory; He closed his eyes, a small fire crackling in a makeshift brazier, with the sparks breaking into the starlit sky, an image of freedom, rising to heaven. Almost in the same thought he knew the answer; he had come too far now to even dare to change his mind.

The fallen leaves rustled underfoot as Bill slowly trod the gravel path towards the cenotaph. A moment later he arrived at an area of neatly cut grass, where, bordered by ornamental bushes and flowerbeds, like a motionless sentinel stood the edifice. He shone his torch on the words inscribed in large letters: The Glorious Dead. Bill approached the low steps; the steps lined with the wreaths that were laid that morning by the Mayor and other local dignitaries.

The fog seemed to be thickening again, wrapping its silken fingers about him.

"What am I doing here?" he whispered to himself. "This was a mistake, I should never have come; it can't change anything."

Yet even as he spoke he knew it was not true. He had had to come. His all consuming, agonising regret was that he had waited so long.

Now must come the moment he had dreaded most of all. Stepping towards the Memorial he shone his torch on the smaller inscriptions, searching the list of names; with a gasp he found Ernie, Tommy, then Jabez, Jacko and Harold – where was Albert? – Ah yes, he was there too. He could feel his heart pounding in his chest.

The distant voices of passers-by on the pavement drifted across to Bill through the fog. Something stirred in his memory; the voices became those of his old friends, he could feel them around him. Their lives, full of innocent expectation had been so short. How in an instant their dreams had been so cruelly destroyed in the mud filled trenches of those foreign fields.

Bill had experienced a feeling that he too was dead, or at least that life in the sense that other people lived it, was for him, over. How could he be alive, enjoy living, when his friends, and so many young men like them had been denied that chance? It was wrong that he should see the sun rise and his heart be warmed by it each morning, when they could not, it was wrong that he should touch and taste and hear the wonders and beauty of the world when they had been cruelly snatched away.

He looked down at the wreaths of red poppies, the blood red blossoms of war, then, straining his eyes upwards through the fog, towards the figure stood high upon the stone plinth: a lone soldier, head bowed in solemn remembrance for those who had paid the ultimate sacrifice.

Something moving on the ground caught his eye. Stooping, he saw it was a stray poppy. He retrieved the paper flower and held it towards the light. Its petals were creased and grubby.

Delicately he straightened out the petals, and wiped away the grime. "The price of poppies lads; and what a price you all paid." Then he cradled the poppy in his large hands, as if protecting it. Suddenly, overcome with emotion his body crumpled and he fell forward onto the Memorial steps, surrounded by the wreaths of poppies. "I never said goodbye lads," he sobbed, "I never said goodbye!"

"Is that you Bill?"

Bill turned his head slowly and looked up. Out of the mist a young man carrying a torch was slowing walking towards him. Bill's face lit up,

"Albert?" he beamed. "Albert!"

"I beg your pardon Sir?"

"Sorry – Ernie – no, Harold?"

The figure approached him, "Are you hurt sir?" The young policeman asked.

"No – no – I'm sorry son," Bill struggled to his feet.

The policeman helped him up. "We'd better get you home, you'll catch your death out here."

From the park gates a horn sounded. It was Paul. A moment later he was at his father's side.

"Thank goodness, you're alright Dad. I was getting a bit worried, you've been so long."

Paul took Bill's arm, and with the constable taking the other, they guided him gently along the path. When they were safely in the car Paul thanked the officer.

"Least I could do, I just happened to be passing in the patrol car and saw a light flashing about by the Memorial, thought it might be vandals." Turning to Bill he said, "I take it you're a veteran of the Great War sir?"

Bill nodded. "I am son, but there was nothing great about that war."

The police man smiled, "Your son here must be proud of you, and your country should be too."

Paul affectionately squeezed his father's hand. "Oh I am officer," he assured him, "very proud. People don't always understand what men like Dad went through, what goes on inside I mean."

Bill said quietly, "I'm glad I came here, and thank you officer for your help, I'm sorry if I caused any trouble."

"No trouble at all Sir." Said the officer "You take care of yourself."

Bill wound up the car window. "Can you hear it Son?"

"Hear what Dad?" said Paul.

"The Last Post." said Bill.

As he looked across to the War Memorial, tears filled his eyes. The spirits of his dead comrades, his brothers in arms were now fading into the past. Bill raised his hand in one final salute. Holding back the tears he murmured softly,

"Time to stand down lads, time to stand down."


The End

# WHERE AM I NOW

I was a soldier, in a strange and foreign land.
While friends fell about me, I still stand,
Among mud filled trenches I walk alone
Where dead and dying, I prayed for home.

And when the light towards me came
I shouted Mother, called out her name.
But she heard me not, she could not see
And I faded to her memory.

But if in time you think of me
Remember well, who I was to be
Your son, your lover your father, your friend
Forget me not; on you I depend.

I lie 'neath mud of some battlefield,
I gave my life, my destiny sealed
With no known grave, for you to weep
If you forget me, I cannot sleep

What I have seen, you will never see
Where I have been you will never be
What I have done you will never do
But what I did was all for you.

For I am the dead of thousands gone
Our names, long forgotten, our lives, done
And all for what I hear you say
So you could live a brighter day.

From that foreign field to cathedral high
With Kings and Poets, now I lie
My battles fought, my war is o'er
An Unknown Soldier of the Great War

©Susan M Cowley
2013.

Printed in Poland
by Amazon Fulfillment
Poland Sp. z o.o., Wrocław